I0549056

TO BE OR NOT TO BE

Sybil Meets a New Great Britain

Sybil Norcroft Book Eight

CARL DOUGLASS

Neurosurgeon turned Author who writes with
Gripping Realism

PUBLICATION
CONSULTANTS
We Believe In The Power Of Authors

PO Box 221974 Anchorage, Alaska 99522-1974
books@publicationconsultants.com, www.publicationconsultants.com

ISBN Number: 978-1-59433-970-7
eBook ISBN Number: 978-1-59433-971-4
ISBN Numbers, Library of Congress Number: 2020948935

Manufactured in the United States of America

DEDICATION

To My Good Wife, Vera.
My Friend and Love of Sixty Years.

BOOKS BY CARL DOUGLASS
Neurosurgeon Who Writes with Gripping Realism

FICTION

Last Phoenix-A Novel of Betrayal and Revenge, A Story of the CIA's Phoenix Program

Gog and Magog—Yawm al-Qiyamah, Yawm al-Din, The Day of Judgment

Sheep Dog and The Wolf-A Story of Terrorism and Response, and the Sheep Dogs Who Protect

Trojan Horse in the Belly of the Beast, Three Books:
- *– Though They Come From the Ends of the Earth-Book One*
- *– Dancing with the Devil-Book Two*
- *– Trojan Horse in the Belly of the Beast-Book Three*

Finders Keepers, Losers Weep-A Novel of Innocence Betrayed and the Search for Restitution

Gog and Magog—Yawm al-Qiyamah, Yawm al-Din, The Day of Judgment

Saga of a Neurosurgeon Series, Six Books:

- *– Young Coyote-Book One: Garven Wilsonhulme's Way to Success-No Quarter Asked and None Given*
- *– Anything Goes-Book Two*
- *– Heaven and Hell-Book Three: Garven Wilsonhulme Takes on All Comers in the Jungle of Modern Competition*
- *– Long Climb-Book Four: Young M.D., Garven Wilsonhulme, Engaged in a Social Poker Game of Winner Takes All*

– *Academia: The Law of the Jungle-Book Five: Surgeon in Training, Garven Wilsonhulme, Fang-and-Claw Competition for Glory*
– *The Vulture and the Phoenix-Book Six: Neurosurgeon, Garven Wilsonhulme, the Final Great Fight*

All in Jest: Renowned Neurosurgeon in the Fight of Her Life

The Mysterious Alexandra Tarasova Yusupov: A Novel of a Woman who was, as Churchill said, "a riddle, wrapped in a mystery, inside an enigma…"

The Rise and Fall of the Fifteenth Caliphate: The CIA Giveth, and the CIA taketh away…

NOVELLAS

Sybil Series

1st Novella-*The End of the Beginning*

2ndNovella- *Uncharted Country, Uncertain Future*

3rd Novella-*Secrets*

4th Novella-*Secrets and Scandals*

5thNovella-*Decisions*

6thNovella-*Running with the Big Dogs*

7thNovella-*Sybil Norcroft Meets the Devil*

8thNovella-*Sybil's Question: To Be of not to Be...*

McGee Series

1st Novella-*Friends at Homeland Security*

2nd Novella-*Crossing the Cult*

3rd Novella-*Wednesday's Child*

4th Novella-*Death on a Pale Horse*

5th Novella-*The Boss's Daughters*

6th Novella—*Another Whistle Blower*

NONFICTION

On Evolution and *Something about Religion*
Both out of print

DISCLAIMER

This book is fiction; the characters are the products of the author's imagination and are not persons who ever lived. Any resemblance to the characters and actual people, or of the story to actual events would be purely coincidental and unintentional.

CHAPTER ONE

Sybil Norcroft remembered well a summons from the President of the United States about six months ago when he delivered a verbal bombshell. She was always ambitious, but the request by President Willets that day was a shock even for the woman of ice who was serving then (and now) as the Director of the Central Intelligence Agency. His precise statement had been, "Sybil, I am all but certain that Randall Broome will be the next president of the United States and Dick Harris his vice-president. I have two secrets I want to share with you since you are my most trusted mistress of the vault of secrets and chief of the puzzle palace."

She had smiled at his characterization of herself and her agency.

He had continued, "What I have to tell you must never be repeated…Harris is very ill, and no one else but Governor Broome and I know that. He just found out two weeks ago, and it is too late to get a new V-P at this late date. The best estimate by his doctors is that the poor man will have to resign for health reasons before the end of his first year in office."

Sybil had digested every word, waiting almost without breathing for the next sentence—the virtual next shoe to drop.

President Willets had not disappointed her, "And Governor Broome himself has mild to moderate congestive heart failure—that's another top secret—his prognosis is not all that good so far as I have been told. I owe him my place in the White House and could never do or say anything that would deny him his chance. He has been a real patriot and has the good of the nation foremost in everything he does."

The president looked directly into Sybil's intent eyes, "He and I have discussed the need for him to appoint you to the vice-presidency when the time comes for Harris to step down."

He paused to allow Sybil to digest the import of what he was telling her.

She remembered saying, "Mr. President, I would be proud to serve. You know I would do anything for you."

She was well known to be a woman who chose her words very carefully and to be a person whose word was her bond, as old-fashioned as that might sound in these unsettled times.

"Thank you, Sybil. I know you would. I am sure that you know—should my expectations come to pass—you will become the first woman ever to serve in that high office, just like you were the first woman to serve as the DCIA. I think it highly unlikely that you will ever be the first lady, but with the conditions of politics and the health of the two aspirants in head of you, it is not outside the realms of probability that you will become the first woman to occupy the west wing as its leader and likely will be the first woman of the nation not so long afterward. I am pretty certain that your political career is not over, my friend."

Sybil remembered that she must have appeared like the proverbial deer looking at approaching headlights, "Who knows about such things, Mr. President, who knows?" was all she could manage that day.

For the next few afternoons, Sybil had used a rare period of relative quiet in the spy world to ponder the implication of the president's information and his offer. She had always been convinced that the vice-presidency was "not worth a bucket of warm spit." [actually, the word V-P John Nance Garner had used was not considered appropriate for polite society]. However, she did feel a strong affinity to the current president and was willing to serve him even in an enervating position if that was what he needed. The dangle of becoming the potential president after next had been tantalizing to her. That she could not deny.

Time and circumstance had changed all of that. A few days after that momentous conversation, the world had all but turned upside down. A craven monster who called himself Beelzebub, burst onto the world stage bring death, destruction, confusion, and eventually chaos. At first, the monster seemed to be a fire breathing alt-right extremist bent on wiping out everyone not like his white supremacist friends and co-conspirators. Then, he morphed into a Stalin-like murderer of capitalists, including among them a majority of Caucasians. Finally, he showed his true colors as a chameleon whose intentional changing from one political or racial persuasion to another concealed a bald-faced greed. He was a terrorist determined to frighten and to hold hostage the powers of the world until they acceded to his demands for treasure beyond the imaginations of Croesus and an intention to gain power beyond what Genghis Khan, Julius Caesar, Joseph Stalin, and Adolph Hitler, combined and being fed a nuclear diet.

The news carried the story of the untimely death of Vice-President Harris in the third month of his tenure which quickly elevated Randall Broome to the nation's number two power chair.

What the public did not know was that Beelzebub was the sitting vice president of the United States, Randall Broome, who had gradually created a secret empire based on blackmail, brazen theft, and corruption of easily led sycophants. Before he could bring about a virtual Armageddon, Sybil Norcroft and her CIA, the FBI, MI-6, the Mossad, and every government and intelligence service worked together to identify, to isolate, and to capture, Beelzebub. Broome was flabbergasted that he had been discovered and so easily brought down.

The meeting today had been requested by President Willets to learn what had become of the currently most hated man in the world, and what the future would hold.

"Sybil," he said, "I think it safe to say that our discussion a few months ago is now moot. Randall Broome will never be president; Dick Harris died in office—maybe he was even murdered to put Broome in his place—and now Broome has left us another politically charged vacancy."

"I don't envy you for having to make such decisions, Mr. President. I certainly won't hold you to anything you suggested back before Broome burst on the scene."

"Thank you, Sybil. Before we get to that problem, tell me what you have done with Beelzebub. I can hardly speak the man's name."

"To this point, the Firm has made every effort to keep his whereabouts—and his very existence—out of the public information domain. We should probably make a final decision today. For the time being, he is in the basement floor dungeon of the top-secret black ops prison in the most guarded area of Camp Peary."

"That's the CIA training center in Virginia that is top secret but everyone in the world seems to know about, correct?"

"Correct."

"How is that spherical S.O.B. doing?"

"He is fine. I have ordered an absolute around the clock suicide watch. He is in a brightly lit double barred cell with no windows. He is naked, being force fed to keep him from starving himself; his food consists of a boring perfectly and scientifically devised, then ground into featureless balls; and he receives a vigorous daily shower and very invasive examination four times a day. He has no radio, television, or reading material of any kind; and everyone attending to him has been ordered to be a deaf-mute and never to look the beast in the eye."

"Does he get exercise?"

"He does. It is very carefully supervised by two full-time navy physicians, an exercise physiologist, and two large and no-nonsense nurses. One is a male body-builder who is in charge of his day to day health care. Incidentally, Broome no more has congestive heart failure than I do. The second is a psychiatric nurse specialist who watches his every twitch to anticipate any suicidal thoughts or actions. She is a world champion MMA blackbelt you would not want to bump into in a dark alley on any given dark night."

"Tell me, how often does he see the natural light of day?"

"Never. He stays in his cell–a room half the size of your bathroom in the White House residence—twenty-ty-three hours a day—then is prodded out to a silo kind of a tower where a couple of unfeeling brutes chase him around and force him to pump iron, do push-ups, pull-ups, and jumping jacks, for exactly one hour by the clock. No more, no less."

"How is his psyche holding up?"

"Pretty well according to Dr. Gabler, the psychiatrist. The man is not a particularly touchy-feely sort of country club doctor, but he is very bright, insightful, and experienced. He is a professor someplace. So far so good; better than Beelzebub the man or the demon of imagination deserves, in my opinion."

"I have given the matter considerable thought. There is an issue of justice; some have guessed that he is alive and will surely be tried in open court. Your deputy thinks he should be given an in-house summary trial in the basement of the Firm's building and returned to his present status for the rest of his life. Any number of my advisors think he should be shot once in the back of the head by a master sergeant with a steady hand who will not waste a second bullet on that waste of air and space."

"What do you think, Mr. President?"

"As I said, I have thought about this. Mr. Broome was in a terrible automobile accident yesterday while traveling in rural upstate New York. He was killed instantly; fortunately, he never suffered. His wife is grief stricken, but was mollified when I told her that he would receive full national honors—flags at half-staff, a flag draped casket in the capitol rotunda for mourners to pass slowly by, then burial of his casket in Arlington National Cemetery. His nice wife and family receive his full pension for life."

"And the man himself?"

"Let him stay exactly where he is. He is to be identified only by number, have no visitors, and no information is to come in to him or out from him or us for the rest of his unnatural life. May he rot. Agree?"

"Emphatically, Sir. In fact, his continuing existence should be a code level secret known only to the presidents and DCIAs to come, and no one else, ever."

"A girl after my own heart, Sybil. Will you give him the good news?

"It will be my decided pleasure."

"Which brings to mind the question: what should be done about you?"

"Is that a real question or just rhetorical, Mr. President?"

"Real. And I consider you to be wise; so, I will give your answer a great deal of weight."

"This is what I think. Broome had and still has a great many admirers and followers who thought he should succeed you as president—whether by constitutional means following your death or by a basically prearranged election. There is more than a whiff of hatred towards me and the other investigators by some alt-righters and far left-wingers who think I was instrumental in a lethal coup. Their loyalty is a base that is unshakable on either wing.

"I hope you will not think me a braggart, Sir; but I believe you should give strong consideration to appointing me to the vice-presidency once the national hoopla surrounding the unfortunate statesman's death has passed. Despite the political ill-will on the fringes, I think the middle will support you in nominating me—a political neutral–then. Anyone else will be problematical. First, because the political factions will fight to the death to get their man in place, and second, because I am privy to secrets they cannot know including your health status."

"I appreciate and value your candor, Sybil. I agree fully with your suggestions. I have something to add."

He paused…a pregnant pause.

Sybil waited. It was for the president to convey what was likely to be a serious secret.

"Sybil. No one else must know, not even my wife. I have carcinoma of the lung, fairly early stages, but spread beyond the point where surgery is an option. The doctors give me somewhere between one and two years. I want those years to complete my presidential goals. I strongly want to hold out for two years. According to the 22nd Amendment of the U.S. Constitution, a president can serve only two terms—or 8 years in office—with one exception. It is possible for a former vice president to serve 10 years as president if he or she succeeds to the presidency upon the sitting president's death while still in office and who has served two years of his or her term. I sincerely want to give you those ten years, Sybil. Accept this as my formal request but keep it quiet for now. We'll let history work out the details."

"I accept, Mr. President. It is beyond my greatest imaginations. I started out as a doctor and sort of slipped into government service. It appears that I am going to make another slip."

They laughed.

CHAPTER TWO

Vice-President Randall Broome's closed and flag draped casket lay in state in the capitol rotunda for three days as mourners and members of his base filed past to pay homage. They decried the premature loss of the stalwart patriot and statesman. Many wept. Flags flew at half-staff all around the capital city and everywhere a federal building stood, and on the front lawns of thousands of homes of the faithful. In his dedicatory prayer, the congressional chaplain praised the beloved man and made mention of how fitting it was that he should be honored in a manner like that accorded first to Henry Clay, then over the years to such presidents as Abraham Lincoln, George H.W. Bush, and notables such as Senator Elijah Cummings, Rev. Billy Graham, and Senator John McCain.

DCIA Sybil Norcroft and President Willets stood close to each other as the chaplain intoned his prayer and struggled to keep their faces free of expressions of smiling or nausea. The funeral was an ordeal for all—the sad wife and two sons, the invited political guests, and the four people who knew what a sham and a disgrace it was.

With the permission of the president, Sybil took a month-long backpacking vacation in the Wasatch Mountains of Utah, above the Brighton and Park City ski resorts. Sybil, her handsome and athletic husband, industrialist Charles Daniels, and her daughter Cerisse and her husband, Drake Farrer. The Farrers had two children, Sybil Aminita, age six, and Drake, age three. They were left at home with their nanny, a woman from the same village in the Congo where Cerisse lived until she was rescued from her French human traffickers. The trip was cleansing and enlivening. Only there in the pristine mountains was Sybil able to let go of the nightmares that were an occupational hazard for a person who knew about, had seen, and was responsible, for things that few people had the stomach for.

Charles was, as always, her rock—the one absolute she could count on in her often chaotic and frequently painful world. They loved one another with both passion and gathering wisdom. When they arrived back in Washington to begin the daily grind again, Sybil paid close attention to her very regular monthly periods because of the freedom she had allowed herself. Another pregnancy would be both a joy and a strain on the Daniels' busy agendas.

As a result of the Beelzebub investigation, chase, and capture, the Russians, Americans, and Chinese, were enjoying the warmest relationships they had had since before the Cold War. President Parker Conrad Willets embarked on a six-week world tour to accomplish one of his life's dreams—that of cleaning up the planet's oceans. He was slated to sign the UNFCCC [Paris Agreement within the United Nations Framework Convention on Climate Change], dealing with greenhouse-gas-emissions mitigation, adaptation, and finance, signed by most developed nations in 2016, including the United States. However, the United States formally withdrew by a presidential order of one of Willet's predecessor, a populist who opposed international agreements in general and those which threatened American business supremacy in particular. It was Willet's career long dream to achieve peace and amicable union between the Peoples Republic of China and the Government of China, Taiwan. It was a very ambitious set of goals, and President Willets' endurance was beginning to wane.

Sybil's day to day task of obtaining cooperation among egocentric organizations was considerably more formidable. She and the DNI David P. Jacobsen were in agreement with each other to get all of the seventeen American intelligence services to participate together instead of giving grudging lip service to the law that required full fealty and cooperation to the ODNI [Office of the Director of National Intelligence]. It had been an uphill battle thus far, but the Beelzebub affair had proved to everyone that cooperation was possible if it was deemed that the stakes were high enough.

Once again, however, hers and Director Jacobsen's plans were derailed by the intrusion of a new international threat. It seemed both absurd and beyond imagination that the newly coined Brexit nation of the United Kingdom should pose an existential problem for the democratic sphere of interest, including affecting America. Benjamin Wood-Jackson, the newly verified populist prime minister of England was protected in his position by an overwhelming vote of confidence by both the rank and file of British Conservative and Tory party aficionados–only one individual voted against the government beginning Brexit for real by invoking Article 50 of the Lisbon Treaty.

The DCIA and DNI began including the UK/EU diplomatic issues in their PDBs [President's Daily Briefings]. DNI Jacobsen—because of his central authority—was the designated spokesperson.

"Mr. President, we have been following the Brexit issues since the beginning. As of Friday, January 31 at 23:00 GMT, the UK officially left the European Union after 47 years of membership, and more than three years after it voted to do so in a referendum. Prime Minister Wood-Jackson held his first cabinet meeting of the new era at the National Glass Center, a museum and arts center in Sunderland, the city that was the first to back Brexit when the referendum results were announced in 2016."

"How has the PM reacted?" President Willets interrupted.

"Publicly, he commented that there is no need for the UK to follow Brussel's rules to have a trade deal with the EU. Privately, he says that he couldn't care less whether or not there is any trade deal. He would be just as happy to "bury them" as have a deal. You might have caught the news on the day Brexit took place. In Brussels, the UK flag was removed from the European Council Building, and Wood Jackson stood up and cheered in a cabinet meeting.

"He has indicated that he might accept a Canada-style free trade deal but would return to the withdrawal agreement if he does not get what he wants."

"I should be asking Secretary Loganshire about these matters of state, but you tell me: how did all of this sit with Michel Barnier?"

"The EU leader privately scoffed. Give me a second to get his exact quote. Here it is. "This is an outlandishly ambitious trade deal for a second-rate country to be demanding. At the very least, we would have to have a level playing field; and I don't think Benjamin Wood-Jackson knows what that means."

"What's your agency's take on what Johnson might actually do?"

"He's a populist; so, all bets are off in terms of cooperation with other countries. He has given any number of speeches in which he insists that England can regain its previous grand status and be great again under his leadership. His fixed bank of supporters has actually increased in the past six months. He tells them that the old alliance with the United States is defunct by agreement between himself and the previous president. The Firm is nearly unanimous that he will mount some trade measures to test the will of the US in confrontations. Secretly, we have good intelligence that he is ordering some anti-American trade hacking operations, both gathering information and some actual cyberattacks."

"Has the man gone nuts?" exclaimed President Willets.

"Not at all. He is what he has always been—a populist, and an extreme one."

"Are we taking adequate note?"

"Yes, Sir, we most definitely are. It is a new world out there. New friends, new enemies, and a playing field that tilts almost monthly."

"Keep me posted on what that loonie does. Maybe, he'll have to be reined in."

Sybil had to make a shift in priorities due to budget cuts. She shifted a few agents from the Russian, Chinese, and terrorist, desks to the England desk and increased the budget in favor of the emphasis on England. That came about because of Johnson's bellicosity, his determination to return the UK to the glory of "*Pax Britannica*", his stubborn obstructionism in negotiations, his insistence that the bilateral military treaty between England and the United States be renegotiated in favor of England, and his insistence that England's debts be forgiven. The government of the United States was developing increasing concern on Johnson's mounting attacks on NATO, the FPDA [The Five Power Defense Arrangements]–a series of defense relationships established by a number of multi-lateral agreements between the United Kingdom, Australia, New Zealand, Malaysia, Singapore, (all Commonwealth members), and the United Nations.

Diplomatically and on trade issues the new PM was becoming increasingly vocal about leaving the United Nations Security Council, a founding member of the G7,

G8, G20, NATO, OECD, WTO, Council of Europe, OSCE, the Commonwealth of Nations, and going it alone. His nativist populism, xenophobia, racism, misogynism, anti-immigration, parochialism, and nationalistic stance, anti-globalization/country-first was beginning to raise flags of concern among developed nations and former allies, especially the United States. These could endanger systems of public education in the West as the rising right-wing fringes on the political spectrum wholeheartedly support privatization of the public good.

Sybil met with President Willets on the eighth day after beginning her agency's surveillance and study of what was beginning to appear like a new United Kingdom under a new, increasingly despotic leader.

"Mr. President, Great Britain's Conservative Party is generally quite moderate but–like the Republican Party in the United States–it must pander to the hard-right nativists within its ranks in a quest for a voting majority. I don't need to tell you that getting re-elected is as primal in England as it is in our country. That moderate policy still maintains British determination that the United Kingdom's relationship with the United States represents Britain's most important bilateral relationship.

"However, the right-wing of the Conservative Party has to struggle with what we would refer to as the alt-right. What separates right-wing populists from the more moderate rightwing establishment is their opposition to the free movement of people, both economic migrants and refugees, across national borders. This is really no different than the many fairly new populist-run countries.

"Nativist movements have historically come from the political right. It follows quite logically for the ultra-right nativists that they must attempt to keep the power, elections, and re-elections, within the dominant culture and race. The white race or tribe all over the world–and now very strongly in the UK–has its nativist populists' hyper-right-wing, and anti-government stances."

"What are the credos of those hyper right-wingers, Sybil?"

"The UK is becoming the loudest and most extreme faster that we would ever have predicted. Among their long and strongly held beliefs is a sense of freedom, particularly freedom from tyranny. That now prevails in the West. But that is to some degree code. I am sure you are aware that the term, 'religious freedom' as used by conservative religious groups is code for 'freedom from gays and gay marriage' and adherence to the anti-LGPTQ-I interpretation of the Bible. Over time, in some areas, this kind of thinking has led anti–social democratic cabals—the objectivists in the US, the hard core rightists in Great Britain which leaned towards Nazism just prior to World War II, and is now seeing a revival of skin-head recruitment and violence. They are opposed to the Keynesian economic policies of controlled capitalism and wish to see almost all government rules and regulation done away with. The UK under Wood-Jackson is taking the reins as a leader of the movement. He is beginning to stand out as the first among equals among such populists as Le Pen of France, Benjamin Wood-Jackson of Great Britain, and Jimmy Åkesson of Sweden, all charismatic leaders in their own right.

"Frankly, it is not much of a stretch to look back into modern history to see the antecedents: think of the notorious and terrible example of nativist populism of Adolph Hitler and his Nazi Party of the late 1920s and 1930s. During those two decades, their propaganda machine made large posters which promised to '*make Germany great again.*' Wood-Jackson's far right constituents—his base, as he calls them–is strutting around with posters telling the British people to '*Make Britain Great Again.*'"

"Are we threatened by that ideology, Director?"

"We are unsure. But, bear in mind that everyone ignored Hitler when he and his brown shirts marched around in military parades carrying brooms and hoes. They could no longer be ignored when those brooms and hoes were replaced by fine rifles. At the same time, Benito Mussolini was attempting to create a 20th-century Roman Empire, and he was written off as a crank and as some sort of a strutting clown. Japanese Emperor Hirohito and his powerful generals were espousing militaristic imperialism while we watched because it was not our sphere of influence. All of which led to World War II.

"You don't really think those fly-by-night populists and their drivel are an existential threat to the United States do you, Sybil?"

"Not now. Very few serious investigators or historians believe that the current spate of populism is as hazardous to the health of the world as Hitler and Mussolini. At this point in time, very few would argue that current populists function at these levels of depravity; but it is no stretch to see that their nativist beliefs are similar to those of their infamous antecedents. The most notable of the over the line populists are the nativist movements growing among the Brexit enthusiasts."

"Do think we should do something?"

"I believe we should wait and watch. For now, the United Kingdom and the United States are close military allies. Our two countries share cultural similarities, as well as military research and intelligence facilities. The UK has purchased military technology from the USA such as Trident ballistic missiles, and the US has likewise purchased equipment from Britain—think of the Harrier Jump Jet. The USA also maintains a large number of military personnel in the UK, and we have a very friendly relationship fostered by our providing a great deal of military training for their armed forces personnel. We should make a kind of quiet red-line. If Wood-Jackson becomes more critical and threatening, and if he decides to oust our personnel from the UK or Europe, or if he makes secret or overt alliances with the Russians or the Chinese, then, I think it will be time to do something. We would be unteachable fools if we let WWIII creep up on us like we did with WWII."

"You know, Sybil. I am getting too old and tired for this. I will not be sad to turn the reins over to you," the president mused, mostly to himself.

CHAPTER THREE

Lincoln Howard and Mac Young—both old stalwart agents of the Firm and entrenched friends of Sybil Norcroft—sat like wooden statues on hardwood straight back chairs in the spacious conference hall in Aston University, Birmingham, England. The event was the CPC [Conservative Party Conference] a four-day national conference event held by the Conservative Party in the United Kingdom every year around October during the British party conference season. The meetings are intentionally held when the House of Commons is in recess. The focal event is the leader's speech which is given by the incumbent Leader of the Conservative Party—presently Benjamin Wood-Jackson–at the end of conference. This year, the Democratic Unionist Party hosted the annual reception at the conference, owing to the recent alliance between the two parties.

The two CIA operatives maintained expressionless facies and never looked at or spoke to one another. Both were recording the prime minister's speech as part of their surveillance and investigation of him and his colleagues.

They were under deep cover and knew that the Firm would deny their existence if they were discovered. It was bad form to spy on one's friends, everyone knows. Their investigation—including some very bad form type hacking—had been underway for six months, and the evidence was accumulating. The spying had now reduced in interest to two individuals, Prime Minister Wood-Jackson and 1SL/CNS [The First Sea Lord and Chief of the Naval Staff] Jonathon Lester-Proxmire, who were the most outspoken of British officials against American interests. Jackson's sycophantic followers had proved to be basically harmless so far as the two American agents, the NSA, and the ODNI, had been able to determine.

Jackson introduced himself, then launched into his fiery speech.

"Fellow real Britishers, I have gotten a great deal done in the past few months, and I want to bring you up to date. Brexit is complete; our association with the EU is past history. Those morons could not see a good deal when it was presented to them in full detail; so, there is not now and never will be a trade deal with those fools. We go it alone as we always have, and we will bury them."

Here, he pounded his fists on the lectern and ran his fingers through his hay-stack of golden hair.

"We are making progress on the immigration problem. We have succeeded in halting the influx of Muslims, and people from the poverty-stricken pseudo-countries who have nothing to offer our *Pax Britannica*. We still have a vexing problem of what to do with that ilk who are already ensconced in our beautiful land. I have some good ideas. I'll let you know when they come to fruition. I am a winner, and I will win this skirmish as well.

"Our base remains steadfast. It has been wise on my part to curry full favor with the main supporters of our party—those called 'nativists' by our detractors. I tell you here and now that I am proud to be a nativist. The white race must be brought back from its minority position, and I am making great headway in that effort. Our economy is beginning to boom, making a great comeback after implementing the changes I initiated. Our large employers are beginning to take on new employees because of my tax breaks. There's a great old saying that speaks truth to what I have accomplished—'What's good for the John Lewis Partnership plc and BP is good for the UK'."

1SL/CNS Lester-Proxmire followed the prime minister, a fairly unusual break in tradition, since, technically, he was not a politician. His remarks were more interesting to the two CIA agents that that of the prime minister because of the greater bellicosity and intensity the influential admiral projected.

"Ladies and gentlemen of the Conservative Party, and fellow patriots. I am an old military man; so, don't be surprised when I am blunt and likely politically incorrect."

The audience guffawed and applauded until their hands were sore. The stubborn old sea-lord was extremely popular with the rank and file of the conservatives and their base.

"We have been playing second fiddle to the United States for far too long. We have been treated like second-class helpers instead of first-class partners. I remember having to sit through a talk by some two-bit American general who said that the British military has nothing left but, 'Generals, admirals, and bands,' and I also recall having to listen to an instructor at the War College tell us about first world war British offensive at Passchendaele in 1917, when General Douglas Haig lost another great battle and another 275,000 troops. The Americans laughed at us about a battle whose name became synonymous with pointless slaughter where 'lions were led by donkeys'. They never let us live that down; so, the phrase came to be associated with the British army. Think how many debacles by the Americans I could list. But we give them a pass because they are our great friends."

The sarcasm was thick.

"Now we have a man as PM who has a spine, who has the courage to lose a few English lives for a God blessed mission. Now we have a government ready to restore our rightful place at the top of the list of nations. Again, we are gathering our forces, and they will command respect. Watch the news, ladies and gentlemen. The Americans will eat their words. They will give us due respect or feel our wrath. The day of us being the dependent weak cousins is over."

Although the admiral droned on for another hour, he gave no details about his great crusade against the dreadful Americans.

Lincoln and Mac followed the crowd out of the hall at Aston University and onto the sunny streets of Birmingham. They walked up the three flights of stairs to their safe-house apartment and sat down at their computers in the thoroughly cybersecure room to send their reports.

Sybil got the gist: "Look for some kind of trouble coming from the UK. Firebrands are beginning to gather."

Sybil and the president gathered in the Oval Office with the Joint Chiefs of Staff, the secretaries of state and defense, the speaker of the house, and the majority leader of the Senate, for a serious discussion of this new and peculiar situation that was arising.

President Willets bade everyone to take a seat, then—wasting no time on preliminaries—said, "As weird as it may seem, we are becoming aware of a threat posed to us by our longest and best ally—Great Britain. Earlier this year when I first got a hint of what was going on in post-Brexit UK, I wrote it off as puffery from extremist blowhards. I am sad to say that the rhetoric has increased and sharpened into oblique threats which are not even kept private in the rooms of the British government.

"Our DCIA can fill us in on the details, such as are available at this time, Dr. Norcroft..."

"I am a student of history; and as such, I am disinclined to ignore bluster from belligerents. I am also not inclined to take protestations of loyalty and undying fealty at voice value. We have paid a dreadful price for such thinking in the past. Need I cite any more examples than Hitler, Stalin, Hirohito, Mussolini, or Al Assad? Our investigations into European digital transmissions and open public speeches cause us pause: the progressively despotic Wood-Jackson government in England has been vociferous in its criticism of all things American and disparaging of our military might. That would give concern enough, but twice in the past week, British vessels have halted and boarded two American vessels. The first was the *Angela-Dorian*, a small cruise ship owned by American Cruise Lines, in international waters between Seattle and Vancouver, British Columbia. The pretext was that we were taking fish from Canadian waters. That was an untruth.

"The second was more serious: *HMS Great Predator*, fired a shot across the bow of the *USS Straits Defender*, an LTS [Littoral Combat Ship], which is a small multi-hulled trimaran/double-outrigger combat vessel on shore patrol duty along the Iranian coast. It was operating in international waters without any doubt on the navy's part. The British navy captain told the skipper of the *Straits Defender*, that his vessel was operating at the behest of the Iranian navy to assist in "halting the provocations by the US Navy against Iran's legal interests". Rather than start an open sea-battle with an ostensible ally, Lt. Cdr. Neal Dastrup, the skipper, allowed his ship to be impounded by the Iranian Navy; and it is being held in Bandar Abbas–a port city and capital of Hormozgān Province on the southern coast of Iran–on the Persian Gulf. The city occupies a strategic position on the twenty-one-mile wide Strait of Hormuz, and it is the location of the main base of the Iranian Navy. It is the port city where previous impounded vessels have been taken. No one was killed or injured; and the US naval personnel are being treated as POWs in strict obedience to the laws of war, according to the International Red Cross, despite no formal declaration of war being in effect between the US and the IRI [Islamic Republic of Iran]."

There was silence in the Oval Office after Sybil's succinct presentation.

Finally, the CJCS [Chairman of the Joint Chiefs of Staff] said, "If ever there was an incident that can be defined without question as an act of war. This is it."

The secretary of state interrupted, "By whom?"

The CJCS did not mince words, "Both."

"An act of war by the UK, by England?!" the secretary exclaimed in disbelief.

"Plain as the nose on your face."

"I'll need more than this presentation to agree that we have just had a true war-like provocation by our longest persisting ally."

"I take it that all agree that Iran has just fired a hostile shot across the bow of an American ship—a piece of territory as American as Boston Commons," said the president.

That was sobering and required a few moments of introspection on the part of everyone in the room before an answer came.

"I'm afraid so," said the secretary of defense quietly.

"Sorry, my fellow Americans, but there seems to be an equal provocation—Great Britain and Iran. What are we going to do about it?" President Willets asked pointedly.

CHAPTER FOUR

Lincoln and Mac waited with baited-breath in the shadows of the Liverpool Cathedral nave. They had lingered in obscure areas until closing time and did not move from their dark places even though no one was left in the huge church presumably. Half an hour passed.

Mac whispered to Lincoln, "Whadda you think? Will he be here or not?"

"Don't know, but we have to be patient. It is too important to miss this chance."

Lincoln heard it first and pointed towards the altar. There it was again—a small sound of stone sliding on stone.

Both men drew their weapons and kept their eyes glued on the area in front of the altar.

In less than a minute, a man's head appeared above the floor, peeking out from a spot in the stone floor where a stone tile had been moved aside. The person—presumably a man—was wearing a black knit sailor's cap. His white skin showed only dimly in the limited light. He pushed his way out of the hole in the floor and began to look around.

"Should we signal?" Mac asked in a very soft whisper.

"Wait. We don't need surprises."

The newcomer seemed to get his bearings and began to walk towards the nave where the two CIA spies were hiding. He was wearing soft soled shoes and made no sound as he crept slowly towards them. After a minute, it was apparent that he was carrying a mat black colored hand-gun.

Mac and Lincoln stiffened.

The newcomer—presumed to be the person they were scheduled to meet—never varied his approach. They had been precise about the meeting place; and Mac and Lincoln were in place, as immovable as the statues of saints around them.

A man's voice came in a whisper, "Peace be unto you, Brother," it said.

"And success in ventures," Lincoln answered back, completing the code and response code agreed upon a week ago in a quick meeting in London.

"Gentlemen," the man said, "thank you for being here in the right place and at the right time. We have to be brief, and we all understand that this meeting never took place."

"Yes, Sir," Mac said. "What do you have for us?"

"Mixed messages. I have copies of several meetings of the Defense Staff. There are direct quotes from General Sir Nicholas Carter GCB, CBE, DSO, ADC, and John Peter Milstrom, the permanent undersecretary. In case you are not aware, Carter is the head of the British Armed Forces, equivalent to your chairman of the joint chiefs of staff; and Milstrom is the defense ministry's senior civil servant, equivalent to your secretary of defense. Other quotes come from staffers, three other generals, and two admirals. Because of the importance of the meeting, Donald Creighton, the queen's private secretary, was in attendance and made the queen's opinions very clear. The quotes speak for themselves and reflect a considerable amount of disagreement among the members. Remember, this is top secret information. If I am exposed, I will be executed. If you are exposed, your country will be humiliated; and you will disappear into the bowels of HMP Bedford never to be seen again."

"Understood. Did you arrange the numbered account in Vanuatu?"

"I did. Here's the account number."

"How do we get out of here before morning?" Mac asked.

"Follow me out. We will disappear into the earth and darkness. I have a torch. That is the only way to find your way through the labyrinth of tunnels."

Lincoln pocketed the information, and the three men moved silently to the secret passage beneath the floor of the cathedral. The visitor moved the heavy stone slab back into place, and the three made their way through the mine-shaft darkness to the center of a sheep pasture to the northwest of the cathedral property. It was dark when they emerged from the tunnel; but there was enough light from the surrounding city to permit the men to separate, and Mac and Lincoln to make their way back to their London safe house without breaking a leg.

Once back in the safety of their run-down flat, the two spies crafted a report to the DCIA and encrypted with an agreed upon one-use code.

To: DCIA
From: Agent 62-AZ7622B and Agent 70-AZ86KB
Status: "Top Secret/SCI" level–access to specific sensitive compartmentalized information included below. Coded, eyes only, DCIA.

Mixed opinions:

[The First Sea Lord and Chief of the Naval Staff] Jonathon Lester-Proxmire expressed great satisfaction about the results of the naval forays in the Gulf of Hormuz and promises more. Authority from PM.

Chief of Defense Staff expressed dismay at the attacks and concerns about expected reply from US.

Permanent Under Secretary John Peter Milstrom, agreed with 1SL/CNS, and cited full approval from PM and Queen's military advisors.

Queen's private secretary Donald Creighton conveyed the Queen and Prince Consort's strong opposition to any further belligerence towards the US.

SIS/MI6 [Secret Intelligence Service] expressed strong positive opinion about the naval incidents and about the general program of disinformation and provocation against the US, stating that the US is in a weakened state following the "Beelzebub" incident.

GCHQ and DI [Government Communications Headquarters and Defense Intelligence] stated that extreme caution should be employed if further incidents are considered.

MI5 [Security Service] stated that the naval incidents were appropriate and adroitly executed and that the successes should invite further ventures by the government, ramping up the seriousness of the activities and the rhetoric accompanying them.

> Foreign Minister Grantland Marsh reported a canvass of developed nations and Middle East nations' foreign ministers and found an eighty-five percent approval rating. Seventy percent suggested further and more aggressive tactics.

The next morning's PDB was arranged at 0600 as an emergency meeting to include the entire JCOS, and their deputies; the secretaries of state, defense, treasury, and homeland security; the heads of all seventeen US intelligence services; the speaker of the house, the majority leader of the senate, and their minority leaders.

Sybil Norcroft presented the status of the nation's security during the past twenty-four hours with only one item on the agenda—the British and Iran question.

"Mr. President, our agents have obtained and confirmed evidence that the government of the UK was directly and purposefully responsible for the attacks on our ships. A defense staff meeting the following day revealed strong opinions both in favor and opposed to the PM's actions—apparently taken without informing other government elected or appointed officials in advance except for the naval personnel directly involved. The documents we received indicate that we can expect negative approaches both on a diplomatic and military level."

The secy of state scoffed, "I don't believe a word. Who's your source, Director?"

"I am not at liberty to reveal my sources."

"You mean, you won't."

"Yes, that is exactly what I mean. It would be inimitable to the security of the United States for me to do so."

"Classified, eh?"

"No, Sir. Top Secret, and above your security clearance, Sir."

"What impudence, young lady," the secretary huffed.

"She is the director of the central intelligence agency of the United States, Mr. Majority leader. In this office, she will be addressed as Madam Director. That is final," the president said in his quietest voice, the one everyone had to strain to hear.

"No, harm intended Mr. President. Just a little joke."

"The last one of its kind."

That was the last word on that subject.

The secy of defense asked, "What is our next step, Mr. President. Do we wait for diplomatic responses, or for further provocations, and to what degree do you want us to retaliate?"

Looking directly at the secy of state, President Willets said, "Have the UK ambassador in my office at 1100 today. You be there as well. If I am not satisfied, he and his senior officers will be ordered to leave the country by 1700 today."

The secretary sputtered but shut up when the president raised his right hand as a stop sign.

"Mr. Secretary and CJCS and JCOS, inform your counterparts in the UK that no British or UK vessel will be allowed through the Straits of Hormuz until we have been convinced that no further incidents will occur—in perpetuity," he said to the stolid faced secy of defense and the joint chiefs.

41

The president looked directly at the CNO, "Admiral, get the NIS [Naval Intelligence Service and the ONI–Office of Naval Intelligence–] on this immediately after this meeting. Get every cough and every fart of every belligerent in both the UK and the IRI from this moment forward."

He looked directly at the Director of the U.S. Defense Intelligence Agency, "General, have the deputy director clear her desk of everything else. Go after the Brits. Pull out all the stops."

In *soto voce*, Secretary of State Beverly Armont Willardson muttered, "What hath God wrought?"

As the leaders filed out of the Oval Office, President Willets gently tapped Sybil's shoulder and mouthed the word "wait" to her. She heeded the hint and stayed on.

"Sybil. I think now's the time. Keep on with your work on the British, but—unless you have very negative feelings—I think it is time for your announcement to take place. Okay with you?"

"You're the boss and the expert on politics. If you think the time is right, then; so do I."

"Come back about three, dressed to the nines. Let's get the announcement out. You can continue as DCIA until you and I find someone who's a good fit. Be prompt, because we have to get this done for five o'clock prime time."

CHAPTER FIVE

The audio emplacements—bugs—were successfully Put into the No. 10 Downing secure room by Lincoln Howard and Mac Young who—for that day, at least—were employed by the electrical workers union and dressed in union prescribed bib overalls. They were ostensibly there to check for listening devices which gave them the perfect opportunity to plant several in small, out-of-the way nooks, crannies, and fixtures. It helped that political journalists from all over the realm were staging a protest in 10 Downing's foyer. For weeks they had been complaining that the PM had changed the location from its usual parliament room to be able to exclude left leaning journalists. Because of the antagonism about No. 10 changing the location of its daily briefings with the prime minister's official spokesman from a room in parliament to Downing Street, even middle road reporters present that day in Downing Street walked out.

The last straw for the reporters came after a junior aide to the Leader of the Conservative Party—PM Benjamin Wood-Jackson—ordered the exclusion of several reporters who favored the Labor Party and its views. The mood of the gathering became heated. When it was clear that the PM was adamant about excluding the "lefties" and "stupid whiners" who criticized the Great Man, every reporter who had gathered at 10 Downing that morning walked out in a huff. The meeting had been scheduled to showcase the UK's trade negotiations with the EU—a potentially very important piece of political news. Reporters from the *BBC, ITV, Sky News, the Daily Mail, the Telegraph, the Sun, the Financial times,* and *the Guardian* were in the exodus. Mac and Lincoln blithely walked away with the loud and angry crowd. It was great cover—invisible in plain sight.

The two CIA agents hurried to their safe house, twiddled a few knobs, and *voila*!, Prime Minister Wood-Jackson's harsh recorded voice boomed into the room.

"Party members and friends [with emphasis on friends from the news organizations who might have lingered], I have to tell you how great our success has been; actually, my success, I have to say in all modesty."

The room laughed appreciatively, and Wood-Jackson led the applause for himself.

"The commies and deep, dark, state connivers have been fomenting riots, impeding the progress of our naval actions, and defaming this government. We can no longer tolerate such disloyalty. You need to know is that the UK does not have a constitution. We have no written con-stitution. England has never had a constitution–written nor otherwise formulated–one of the few countries of the world that does not have a written constitution. In the wisdom of our forefathers, we have something we call an 'uncodified constitution'.

"Beginning on Monday next, our armed forces will conduct a two month long military exercise on our soil which will be obscure in its purpose, but it will be an exercise of 'what if a foreign power, or a power hungry UK group' sought to take over the government."

He looked out over the rapt crowd and actually winked at them. He gave them one of his very fetching patented full toothy smiles.

"We are friends here, and we are all in agreement. Anyone who has not been agreement with our plans has long since vacated the government. So, I can tell you—in all confidence—about our actual goals because you are going to be part of them, my loyal base.

"We do not have a constitution to hamper us, but we do have laws—some of them being of my creation—that enable us. We can, and we will, suspend the national laws and such archaic provisions as habeas corpus. And, we will do it one week from today. We will start by conducting urban warfare exercises in all of our major cities to identify and capture the dissidents and take those hordes...and I do mean 'hordes' and haul them off to the hoosegow. These exercises will be a dress rehearsal for the imposition of martial law. It will happen so quickly and subtly, that the poor uneducated schmucks and Muslims and Hindus won't know what has hit them until it is too late. Our world has grown to be too unstable for the hodgepodge of laws we now have to keep us secure. We will have one law and one government, and it will be run by We the People—people being defined as the white, AngloSaxon, Protestant, solid, native Brits."

There were a few furtive uncomfortable glances from some of the older men before the roof rocking applause began.

"We are going to become a nation of armed citizenry just like the Americans. Of course, we will define who does and who does not get to own or carry a firearm. What does it mean for us to suspend rights? It means we will choose. No more dissidents or whining left wing hand wringers. We cannot have our society decay from within any longer. We will declare a national emergency, and we will define 'emergency'; and we will—maybe I should be frank here—*I* will make a declaration about how long the 'emergency' will last. Our law enforcement officers will be deputized as military conscripts. They will round up the subversives like all of the rag-heads, and we will intern enemy nation diplomats. Our bobbies will go house to house confiscating firearms, ammunition, and food supplies."

"Will we need to make a vague notification suggesting of something like a foreign nuclear threat, Mr. Prime Minister?"

"Well, bless the pointy little head of the MP from Manchester Withington. You are right on. Every government agency will act in accordance with that concept. Incidentally, I came up with it last week when this meeting was in its planning stages.

"Under Plan SAVE ENGLAND FOR ITS TRUE CITIZENS, MI-5, Scotland Yard, and the British Army, will be in charge of maintaining law and order, taking charge of resettlement operations, and getting things done, including managing the detention program, much like we did when we had to deal with the IRA during the time of The Troubles. Under The Plan, MI-5 will act on my orders in case of an armed attack or rebellion or even if there is a threat of one in accordance with the Security Service Act of 1989 so long as I deem that those enemies of the people—foreigners, the press, and foreign diplomats–present a serious threat to the internal security of the country. We already know most of the names and bios of the 72 types of undesirables."

"Mr. Prime Minister, can you give us some idea of what kind of people are listed as 'undesirables'?"

"I have been pretty clear on that subject since before I was elected with the largest voting margin in the history of the country: the ultra-left who believe in conspiracy theories that disrespect the government and me; those immoral creatures who believe in abortion, globalism, communism, socialism, same sex love, and the so-called, 'New World Order'. Not our kind of Tory people. That will include most of the Labor Party and its hangers-on like the old Liberal Party, the commies, of course; and any Nazis who have pledged their allegiance to Germany. I have no problem with our home-grown bunch of Brown Shirts. I think they are patriotic citizens myself.

"One last thing I'll tell you; and this is top secret. The Official Secrets Act applies. Once we have our lefties under control, we are going to test the Cousins a bit harder to see what they'll tolerate and what they're made of. All I can say about that part of the plan is that it will make the news."

His speech droned on for another hour and a half. Mac and Lincoln fought to stay awake, but no matter; they had a verbatim recording of his remarks which was automatically being transcribed into code to be sent on to the DCIA. The tired party functionaries and members of the political base walked out of the front door of No. 10 Downing street donning their crisp new black "Make England Great Again!" Caps.

Not much shocked or dismayed Sybil Norcroft, but she was pretty much convinced by now that our old allies had taken a deep dive to the right and were becoming more of a considered national threat to the United States every day when the information came into her hands from Mac and Lincoln. There had been two more naval incidents, during the previous ten days and a land incident in the Falklands where two US service men were injured in a fight with a large number of belligerent British Marines, arrested, and summarily thrown into the clink.

Sybil called the president's appointments secretary.

"I have to see the man PDQ. We have an emergency on our hands, Neva."

President Willets picked up the red phone almost immediately.

"What?" he asked.

She gave him the short but to the point version and could hear him make small gasps.

"Do you think this is accurate? Does the man really believe he can provoke us into a real attack and come out on top?"

"The only thing I can guess about him is that he is a genuine dyed-in-the-wool populist who apparently believes his own malarkey. And, in case you are asking, I do think the man is drifting over the edge into psychosis. Whether he is or not, it seems apparent that he is going to keep ratcheting up the harassment until he crosses a line we can no longer tolerate, and we have to enter into an armed conflict with our longest and strongest ally."

"Do you have a solution to suggest, My friend?"

"I have been mulling one over for the past few days. I don't think you'll like it much, but it might be better than the rest of the alternatives."

"Hold that thought, Sybil. I need to go first. We have been without a veep for quite a while, and it is obvious that we need a good strong one. I need one, and that one is you. I want to make the announcement tomorrow night and at the same time to lay out some areas of real power for you. I have in mind a vice-president on the order of George Bush's Dick Cheney. What do you think? Does that seem to be okay with you?"

"Yes, Mr. President. I want to be right there with you as the fight heats up."

"That's the spirit I like about you, Sybil. We'll go get 'em starting tomorrow after the evening news."

CHAPTER SIX

President Willets had his communications director procure a one-hour spot on every station at six o'clock EST, right after the regular nightly news. The White House clamped the lid on, and there was not a single leak before the witching hour of six arrived. The president sat comfortably in his favorite swivel chair in the Oval Office behind the double pedestal partners' Resolute Desk. The desk was made from the oak timbers of the British ship *H.M.S. Resolute* as a gift to President Rutherford B. Hayes from Queen Victoria. It had appeared on hundreds of television presentations and in innumerable still photographs. A small crowd of dignitaries gathered in the room out of the view of the television audience. DCIA Sybil Norcroft found a folding chair in the back and watched the preparations for the television program about to be announced. Other than the president, she was the only person in the room who was aware of what the purpose of the president's broadcast was.

The lighting camerawoman raised her right hand with three fingers spread. She nodded to the president then began to drop a finger one per second…three, two, one. She nodded and President Willets began to speak.

"Mr. Chief Justice, Speaker of the House, Majority leader of the Senate, my fellow Americans, and distinguished guests. It is my pleasure to present my nominee for vice-president of the United States. As you are aware, it has taken considerable time and a great deal of research to make this selection. This afternoon, Director of the Central Intelligence Sybil Norcroft was presented to the Senate for advice and consent to assume the second highest office in the nation. After a short debate, Director Norcroft, was approved by a vote of 99 to 1. It is with pride that I present her to all of you here in the Oval Office today, and all around the world. The Chief Justice of the United States will administer the oath."

Chief Justice Chester Whitfield rose from his chair and walked to the center of the room directly in front of the center camera. He beckoned, and Sybil walked to the front and stood facing the Chief Justice of the Supreme Court. He was pleased with himself that he had remembered to bring his Bible and a copy of the oath to be administered.

He mouthed the word, "ready?"

She nodded and placed her hand on the Bible.

"Repeat after me, please: "I, *state your name*, Sybil Norcroft Daniels…"

She did so, using her married name of Daniels per her preference.

"I, (state your name), do solemnly swear and affirm that I will support and defend the Constitution of the United States…"

Justice Whitfield lost his place on his card with the written oath.

Sybil continued as if she was repeating after Whitfield… "against all enemies, foreign and domestic; that I will bear true faith and allegiance to the same;"

Without breaking cadence, Whitfield regained his place on the card and continued…"that I take this obligation freely, without any mental reservation or purpose of evasion; and that I will well and faithfully discharge the duties of the office on which I am about to enter. So help me God."

Sybil repeated the justice's words, and the administration of the oath was completed.

"Thank you so much, Sybil, Whitfield whispered. "Old age getting to me."

They smiled at each other, then, there were congratulations all around.

The room cleared, and the president nodded for the crowd to disperse and for Sybil to stay.

"Glad we're through that," he said. "Sybil, I need you to stay on as the DCIA for a bit. My first two nominees refused me. Seems, they got a glimpse of what the DCIA's responsibilities are, and their families wanted none of it. Your husband is a good man."

"He is. I will be glad to help wherever I'm needed."

"Thanks, and apropos. You need to get back to Langley without attracting attention. Two of your agents need to have a serious talk with you. Get back to me, if I need to know about it."

The entire process had taken place over less than an hour, including the exuberant embraces from her good husband and daughter and fine son-in-law. She had been gone from her Langley office for sixty-five minutes.

When she arrived back on the seventh floor of the H.W. Bush CIA Building, Mac and Lincoln congratulated her and got right to the point,

"Sybil…"

"It's Madam Vice-President now, dummkopf," Mac said giving Lincoln a stern look.

Sybil laughed and was joined by her two most trusted agents. The ice was broken, and all three were glad that their close personal arrangement had not been lost. Sybil Norcroft had not forgotten who she really was, and she did not have to make a thing out of becoming the VP.

"Back to business," she said.

Lincoln nodded to Mac and said, "Sybil, our message is Top Secret, plus, plus, plus. Our most trusted asset in the UK's life depends on absolute secrecy."

She nodded her understanding.

"Our asset has an A+ rating, and both of us will attest to his courage and truthfulness. As you know the Brits have been ratcheting up their harassment of our ships. You also know that Mac and I have been listening to streams of information coming from Number 10 Downing. The PM seems to have had no instruction of security of conversations, and he blabs to everyone who comes into his private office—'brags' is the precise word—that the British navy and marines are going to launch a real attack this week that will teach us a lesson. We learned all of that from our listening devices, but we couldn't get anything on the actual target."

Lincoln took over, "Look, Sybil, our asset told us last night that the PM and The First Sea Lord and Chief of the Naval Staff Jonathon Lester-Proxmire have decided that the first target will be NNSY [the Norfolk *Naval Shipyard*, actually located in Portsmouth, *Virginia*]. The chief of construction told us that the new *Donald J. Trump* carrier is ready for christening. The ceremony will take place this coming Tuesday. The breaking of the sacrificial bottle of champagne over the bow is set for 1100 hours sharp. We are aware of several known British naval agents being seen in or near the Navy Yard this past week. Our asset assures us that the Navy Yard is the place—rated 97% certain. Almost a 100,000 people will be there because of the huge popularity of the name of our newest and largest ship. It is a target that could be considered medium soft, and of very high propaganda value."

"Do you really believe that the two main leaders of our once greatest ally are planning to perpetrate an attack on the United states comparable to Pearl Harbor or the Twin Towers?"

"I hate to say it, Madam Vice-President, but our intelligence is too good and too well vetted to ignore. I don't know if you are aware, but Prime Minister Benjamin Wood-Jackson is—at this very moment—sitting in your outer office. He is PO'ED and looks like he is loaded for bear."

"Go out the back door and make yourselves obscure for half an hour. I'll call you on my secure office mobile when I want you back here. This is going to be a busy day."

When the door closed behind them, Sybil buzzed for her secretary.

"Maria, is the prime minister of England waiting out there?"

"Yes, Madam Vice-President. He looks mad enough to spit fire."

"Excellent. Have him wait for five more minutes then show him in. Be overly courteous; smile very *very* pleasantly all the time."

"Yes, Ma'am; it'll be tough; but I'll do my best."

The five minutes dragged by. Sybil swigged down eight ounces of flavored water, checked her nails, made sure her working black shoes looked perfectly shined, then buzzed Maria to bring the nice PM in.

Prime Minister Benjamin Wood-Jackson stormed into the office, his eyes glaring; his smile was a snarl; and his face was red. He was fuming.

"What is the meaning of this delay? For that matter, why am I here seeing a pipsqueak like you?" he demanded.

"I don't know Mr. Prime Minister, why are you here?"

He cursed at her.

She smiled blandly

He asked, "Do you know who I am, young lady?"

"I do. You are Benjamin Wood-Jackson."

"I'll have you know, Dummy, that I am the head of the Conservative Party of the UK—that's in England, presuming you don't know. I am also the prime minister of the United Kingdom. I am here to see the President of the United States for a face-to-face discussion. I will have nothing less!"

Sybil waited, her face a mask of equanimity.

"Well?"

"Well, what?"

"Listen to me, little *bint*. You can't possibly be as dumb as you look and act. I see the president now, or I'm gone, and you will regret it for the rest of your natural life."

"I take that as a threat, Mr. Prime Minister. That piece of slang is inappropriate everywhere in the English-speaking world. You are speaking to the vice-president of the United States. There are policies of decorum even for persons of your ideological persuasion."

"Listen, Sybil, you *wanker…*"

"No, you listen. I am not an idiot; I am the vice-president of the United States. You have not been given permission to insult my office by assuming the privilege of addressing me by my Christian name. You will address me properly as 'Madam Vice-President' or our meeting is over. Do you understand me? If not, I can repeat myself and talk more slowly."

Her voice was her most pleasant and mellifluous. She smiled pleasantly and looked him directly in his eyes.

The fury in the man's eyes was so extreme that Sybil half expected him to jump across the desk and to assault her. She assumed that the only reason he restrained himself was the presence of the 285 pound, six-six, lean with chiseled muscles, black man in the obvious Secret Service suit who leaned towards him as Wood-Jackson's anger mounted.

With tremendous effort, Wood-Jackson fought for control over his emotions. Evidently, his anger management therapy had been for naught.

After a pause of three minutes, he said, "I be-e-g your pardon, MADAM VICE-PRESIDENT," he said dragging the title out as if he were talking to a deranged person who had just named herself "Queen of the May".

"Where is the president, and why am I not sitting in his office talking man-to-man as equal top leaders?"

"I presumed my secretary had already informed you. President Willets has a more pressing engagement. He sends his deepest regrets."

"Listen, La…, Madam Vice-President, I have an intelligence service the equal of yours. I happen to know for a fact that he is touring the Washington zoo with some raghead at the moment."

Sybil shuffled the papers on her desk.

"Oh, yes," she said…"a very important high level discussion with Hamad bin Isa bin Salman Al Khalifa, King of Bahrain."

"Do you know how big that two-bit little country is… you, you…*Vice-President*?"

"I do," she said with calm aplomb. "The independent Kingdom of Bahrain is 782 kilometers square."

He looked at her with the hatred that only the truly ignorant reserve for their betters. He knew that he had been thoroughly one-upped, and he dared not to make a challenge for fear of giving another excuse for the woman to treat him with scorn.

He started to speak, but only emitted a sputter which added further injury to his fragile machismo driven psyche.

Sybil spoke directly to his face: "Mr. Prime Minister, enough chit chat. You are here to talk to me because the president of the United States will not meet you, will not talk to you, will not communicate with you or your government as long as you are in power. To date, your navy has launched unprovoked, and unwarranted attacks on our navy, i.e. on American soil as it were."

He started to speak, but she gave him the benefit of one of her glacial looks—one of those that earned her the reputation of being the Ice Queen. One man who had earned such a glance described it afterwards by quoting Samuel Taylor Coleridge from his ballad, *The Rime of the Ancient Mariner.*

"Day after day, day after day,
We stuck, nor breath nor motion;
As idle as a painted ship
Upon a painted ocean."

"Water, water, everywhere,
And all the boards did shrink;

Water, water, everywhere,
Nor any drop to drink."

"With throats unslaked, with black lips baked,
We could not laugh nor wail;
Through utter drought all dumb we stood!
I bit my arm, I sucked the blood,
And cried, A sail! a sail!"

"Are those her ribs through which the Sun
Did peer, as through a grate?
And is that Woman all her crew?
Is that a DEATH? and are there two?
Is DEATH that woman's mate?"

"Her lips were red, her looks were free,
Her locks were yellow as gold:
Her skin was as white as leprosy,
The Night-Mare LIFE-IN-DEATH was she,
Who thicks man's blood with cold."

He was chilled, and he thought better of speaking. The woman looking at him was a force, a power to be reckoned with. He had nothing to say anyway, really.

"We will have recompense. Count on that. If you persist, recompense will become retribution. If you go through with your plan to bomb an American ship of the line in a naval shipyard crowded with innocents, that mistake will mark your administration forever; and your small and dependent nation will go the way of the Germans, the

Japanese, the Italians, Franco's Spain, and a host of small countries altogether like England who got in the way.

"You have been warned, Sir. Go home. Rethink your folly. We will be waiting. If you come, there will only be one battle. In a few days, there will not be enough of you remaining to mount a second battle. This time, there will be no Marshall Plan."

"Madam, you don't…"

"Shut up and get out or I will have you shackled and dragged to an old cargo ship for delivery to your Labor Party friends with a full explanation of your vicious plans."

Sybil turned her back on him and walked out of the rear door of her office leaving him alone.

CHAPTER SEVEN

Now that Sybil was the vice-president, two things changed for her. First, she had to help in finding her replacement as director of the Central Intelligence Agency; and second, she had to putter with the constitutional responsibilities of her being the vice-president. Those duties took her away from real work, and her first love and loyalty was to the Firm where she was out of the limelight and into the nitty-gritty of making a difference for the country. Lastly, she fretted that she had not completed her last major intelligence mission—that involving the former ally and now at best a superficial frenemy—as a result of the grandiose ambitions of the populist at the head of the government.

She and the president were of one mind about how things should be handled for the time being, given that they had apparently averted an outright and obvious act of war by the growing despot. They both knew that PM Wood-Jackson had only been temporarily diverted from perpetrating an outright attack by being brought up short by Sybil in her office. He had said as much with his parting threats.

Lincoln and Mac were still fully engaged in the tasks of recruiting agents and obtaining intel about what the PM might be planning. The two CIA spies had made a strong bond with a new, and very senior government official who was terrified for his country. He freely spied on the PM and his cabinet and on the senior military officials associated with them. He had surreptitiously recorded an in-camera speech by Wood-Jackson to his cabinet and to several very wealthy cronies from the UK business world. Lincoln and Mac sent a verbatim transcript to Sybil and to the new DCIA designate, with Sybil and the president's approval.

> To: DCIA, POTUS, CJCS
> From: Agent 62-AZ7622B and Agent 70-AZ86KB
> Status: "Top Secret/SCI" level–access to specific sensitive compartmentalized information included below. Coded, eyes only, DCIA, POTUS, CJCS

> "All right, my friends, this is how things stand. I don't who or how, but we have a mole who is betraying our most secure intelligence—probably a far leftie deep stater or some old guard dyed-in-the- wool America friend *über alles*. Whatever, he or she will be found and executed sooner or later. All is not lost. America and its moron president and flutter brained CIA chief have been lulled to sleep and presume that the major attack is not going to take place. Their intel does not match our MI-6 and never has. I will share this with you and only you who are my truly loyal followers: The bombs will explode, but this time, there will not be the slightest

hint or evidence that Britain was involved. We have made mutually profitable arrangements with a couple of hold overs from the Beelzebub group and with Hezbollah who needs to stack up a few more suicide bomber martyrs for their own publicity purposes. The trap is well set and ready to spring tomorrow at 11:30 hours during the CNO's boring speech. In a week, the American fools and the raghead extremists will be at war and doing our work for us."

It took only three secure telephone calls to tighten security at NNSY [the Norfolk *Naval Shipyard*, actually located in Portsmouth, *Virginia]*. The three calls were to: the admiral commanding the new—as yet unchristened]–*Donald J. Trump* carrier; to base security at Joint Expeditionary Base, Little Creek/Fort Story; and Northwest Naval Security in Chesapeake, Virginia. So far as the United States government was concerned, everything had been done that could be done short of a pre-emptive strike on London. Now, they could only wait.

Three overweight ship builders dressed in greasy coveralls, heavy steel toed boots, and hardhats showed up five minutes before check-in time and punched in their cards. No one recognized them or paid the least attention. New guys came and went like a revolving door all the time. Nothing about them drew any attention. They split up. One went directly to the massive new ship, showed his ID, and walked down the three ladders to the engine room where he set up his time-worn tools in the unmanned machinery space—fitted with sensors and control systems to monitor and respond to machinery operating conditions without the necessity of being manned at all times. He was quick and efficient as he deftly exchanged one part for another. The new part was somewhat bulkier and had two cylinders of nearly fluorescent green liquid attached with an assortment of wires to the main frame. He packed up the old part and his tools and left the engine room the same way he had come in. He never spoke a word to anyone.

The second of the three new guys was a carpenter/electrician. He walked to his assigned job for the day—to assure that the loudspeaker system functioned without the slightest annoyance to the tens of thousands of guests and dignitaries. He carried an extra-large wooden carpenter's toolbox with a hardwood handle. There was a large assortment of tools, drop-cloths, and electrical equipment, as well as hammers, saws, and fasteners. Like his co-worker on the ship, his task took little time or energy. He walked all around the reviewing stand and inspected it with great care. He tightened a few bolts, checked stairs for stability, and took a few minutes to exchange the main electrical box for the center loudspeaker with a newer, cleaner, and more streamlined device. He tested the device with his automobile test kit—at least made a point of pushing buttons and writing notes. He then quickly soldered three wires—red, green, and blue—to the inner wall of the new electrical box, admired his work, packed up his gear, and left without his presence being noted.

The third new workman of the day walked purposefully to the temporary security shed set up in the northwest corner of the celebration area bearing a set of four cardboard boxes marked "Naval Vessel Siren System, Type USN 72, Cat. X55" and a collapsible four step ladder. He checked the shed for the best place to attach the contents of the four boxes; and finding four desirable positions, he marked them with a carpenter's broad pencil and set about removing the contents from their cardboard containers.

The security shed was the busiest place in the entire area. Security officers from NCIS, Chesapeake and Norfolk police departments including SWAT; Naval and Marine military police; FBI Rapid Response; Diplomatic Guard Corps; Naval shipyard security details; security from Joint Expeditionary Base, Little Creek/Fort Story; Northwest Naval Security; and more than a few rent-a-cops. Finally, one of the FBI special agents queried the new workman, inspected his boxes and their contents, bade him a good day, and went on to more important security tasks. The SAC and his fellow agents considered it their task to bring order to the security chaos and to be sure they did not act like the Keystone Kops if an emergency did arise. They were determined to make their operation look less like a Charlie-Foxtrot than it did at the moment.

The sirens did not look like sirens. They looked like shiny red metal bricks with a myriad of wires attached to two compact MK 12 Volt, 55 Amp sealed light duty AGM batteries. The contents of the sealed boxes were presumed to be battery parts. No one noticed them enough to ask.

The crowds began to move into the celebration area at the same time the three new workmen walked out of the security perimeter and into obscurity. The security forces were on full alert. Stationary sentries ringed the perimeters. Mobile officers moved in an orderly pattern mingling with the crowds looking for suspicious behavior, attire that looked like coats covering suicide vests. Sgts-major and Master Chiefs checked everything and everyone that did not look like a patriotic, red-white-and-blue loving true American. There was a conspicuous dearth of other types. By 10:45, every inch of the place had been walked on, looked at, or touched, at least twice. The reports to the security shed base were uniformly boring, "all clears".

Chesapeake PD sergeant, Chet Atwood II saw something odd at 10:48 and reported it to his captain.

"Capt. Rich, I'm over by the band stand or whatever they call it. I think you need to come and check out the main loudspeaker. Something's off. Not sure what."

Captain Walter Rich brought along his bomb squad section chief, Randy Markham. The cops squinted for a few minutes at the anomalies pointed out by Sgt. Atwood.

Randy Markham made the initial and salient observation, "That box is too new, has too many wires, and is entirely out of place or my name is not Randy."

Captain Rich made rapid decisions: "Randy or whatever your name is, get the bomb squad over here on the double. Chet, get a squad and clear the area. I'll put out the word to the security heads. Let's get a move on!"

Within minutes the ceremonial stand was swarming with security officers. Randy Markham and his bomb squad had two tall ladders up and were tinkering with wires and connections of the box. Security staff informed the president and the Admiral in charge of the festivities.

While Randy got the red box device down, FBI agents organized a grounds search. NCIS moved onto the *USS Donald Trump* in force evacuating the entire vessel in a few minutes. Then the NCIS special agents, base shore patrol, and ship's security, began a top to bottom, side to side, and floor to ceiling of every space on the ship. They were all sweating with exertion, nervous tension, and pre-battle anticipation by 11:15.

The Master Chief of the Ship, Erik Daniels, made a quick suggestion.

"Agent Parkham, the best three places to plant a bomb on a ship are near the armory, fuel dumps, and in the engine rooms."

"Great thought, Master Chief. Lead the way, and we'll follow."

A dozen noncoms and agents scoured the armory and nearby fuel containers. They came up with nothing. Frustration was mounting to a fever pitch.

The skipper informed the security staff in their shed, and they informed POTUS and the CJCS. The president muttered that he was within five minutes of evacuating the entire festival area and abandoning the ship to any fate it might suffer. The huge number of casualties, especially the innocent civilians, if a massive explosion occurred was a catastrophe no presidential administration could survive.

The Master Chief Engineman greeted the investigators and ordered his crew to attention.

"Master Chief, we have a bomb on board this ship. Most likely place is in this engine room. Find it!"

The Master Chief did not even have time to speak.

EN 1ˢᵗ Class, Dwayne Winters blurted, "I think I know where it is."

As many of the investigators as could fit, ran to the unmanned machinery space following Winters.

"There," he said pointing at the strange bulky electrical box with two cylinders of nearly fluorescent green liquid attached with an assortment of wires to the main frame device of the central engine room control panel.

Every man in the engine room's face went pale, even the African-Americans.' How had they missed it; who put it there and when; and who was going to take the blame? For a moment everyone seemed to be stupefied.

Then, Master Chief Daniels assumed control. He rattled off orders to get the disaster control unit down there on the double. He ordered the men who did not know how to deal with bombs to take charge of removing every sailor off the ship to safety, even the admiral. Men packed the engine compartment with bomb proofing. Men who had to have been crazy when they signed up for such frightening duty, began to probe and test the device. It took fifteen agonizing minutes to remove the bomb, place it in a heavy lead lined box, and for four powerful young sailors to haul it up the four sets of ladders and out into a waiting bomb securing pod on a protected truck. It sped away to the outskirts of Naval Air Station Oceana, Virginia–the home base of SEAL team 6–where it was safely exploded.

The security officers reported to their base and thence to POTUS, VPOTUS, and CJCS.

President Willets heaved a sigh of relief. Sybil was not so sure. POTUS overrode her request that the festival be cancelled and ordered heightened security but did not want to throw a wet blanket on the beautiful and auspicious day.

CHAPTER EIGHT

There were two explosions. They were timed so closely together that most observers thought they heard only one. The first consisted of six simultaneous blasts that completely disintegrated the temporary security staff headquarters in the northwest corner of the NNSY. Fortunately–if such a tragedy could be thought of that way–only nine security men and two women died in the explosion. None of their DNA was every retrieved. The second explosion—actually two simultaneous ones—took place at the opposite end of the Norfolk Naval Ship Yard. After action reports quoted witnesses who saw two suicide bombers blow themselves up—the only good news of the day. Again, the casualty list was low because most of the spectators were gathered around the bandstand at the time.

The presidential historian recorded the moment the group of officials gathered in the Oval Office first learned of the explosions. President Willets was absolutely apoplectic. His face turned purple. He pounded both fists on the Resolute Desk so fiercely that the other men and women in the office worried that he would break his hands; or worse, that he would have a stroke or a heart attack.

Sybil rushed to his side and checked his pulse; it was stratospheric. She pulled him to a couch and shouted for the secretary to bring in the doctor bag. His blood pressure was 190/90. She forced him to lie down and called for the presidential doctor.

Doctor Nichols gave the president a mild sedative—flu-azepam, a fast acting, short duration benzodiazepam–which promptly calmed his rage to the point that he again had control of himself. Doctor Nichols took another blood pressure; it had dropped to 150/86, still high, but only twenty systolic points above President Willet's normal pressure.

He forcibly calmed himself, waited a full five minutes, then said, in a quiet firm voice, "They have actually done it. God save us all."

To the CJCS, he ordered, "Admiral, act with all due haste. Send carrier strike groups: CV-1, 2, 3, and 4 [Lead ships, Langley, Lexington, Saratoga, and Ranger] and block-ade London. They are on Def-con 2 level. Do not fire unless fired upon, but do not hesitate to defend against any attack with maximum prejudice. Put as many ships of the line at sea to interdict any and all travel by British war ships. Board any ships encountered and impound them. If they resist, sink them. Put all other military personnel on Def-con 4; concen-trate on England and Europe. Do not enter into negotiations other than to accept surrender of the opposing force. Leave the general surrender to the president. However, do send a crisp FYI to Andover, Portsmouth, and High Wycombe."

To the secretary of state, he ordered, "Communicate with 10 Downing, the leader of the house of lords, to our ambassador and theirs, and the office of the Queen about the actions we are taking and why. Dismiss the entire diplomatic corps of the UK and list them as *persona non grata*. Do it today. Prepare a written document, and do not permit discussion. This is information, not a diplomatic chitchat."

To the press secretary, President Willets ordered, "Call in the corps for an emergency session to take place one hour from now. Inform them in exact terms who attacked us, where, why, and what we are doing about it. Include the Def-con 2 status; insist that we do not intend firepower retaliation unless we are subjected to further attack. No diplomatic interchange is taking place and will not be resumed until and unless the belligerents cease, desist, and make reparations. Do not; I repeat, do not, accept questions. Speak slowly and precisely and let that suffice. Give the news outlets a headline: Great Britain Attacks US Naval Base Unprovoked!"

DEFCON: The Defense readiness Condition. DEFCON 2 is high readiness; armed forces ready to deploy in six hours.

He indicated that the meeting was adjourned by a wave of his hand, "Now, let's all get to work. VP Norcroft and Gen. Zabriski, please stay for a couple of minutes more."

He posed a question to his most trusted confidants–the VP and his chief of staff, "Speak candidly. Was I a chicken and too timid? or was I too hawkish and will provoke an all-out war as stupid as World War I?"

Gen. Zabriski was a man of few words after a thirty-year career as a battlefield commander, "Mr. President. They have not suffered enough, not anything really. Some real—even if small—damage needs to be inflicted."

Sybil sighed, "I agree with your present plan as a preliminary. If we encounter verbal belligerence from the fool at 10 Downing or physical belligerence from them anywhere in the world or in any form, then, it is my counsel that you order a rapid response, starting small and rapidly escalate if as long as we meet resistance. We must act quickly and decisively on all fronts if we are to avoid a true war. Diplomatically, it's all hands-on deck to spread our gospel. We are innocents who have been stabbed in the back by a dictator in the making. Be free in conveying the evidence except for doing anything that compromises our agents. Get Congress on board with a secret Declaration of War prepared and ready."

President Willets nodded, put his elbows on the desk and templed his fingers on the bridge of his nose, "All right, summon everyone to the war room."

Sybil cancelled all her appointments for the next three days; and, after the war room meeting, she went to ground to organize the intelligence response in conjunction with the ODNI. The first order of business was to make contact with Mac and Lincoln on the secure and encrypted line.

"You have no doubt heard about the attack?"

"Yes, we did. The news is all out in the open, at least what Benjamin Wood-Jackson wants everyone to know.

He shouts his own praises to everyone who will listen and brags about the 'conclusive strike by the armed forces of the UK against the tyrannical enemy'. The nation has been placed on high alert, and bomb shelters have been activated."

"What about the people on the street. What's your take on their perception of what is going on?"

"Generally, glum. A few of Wood-Jackson's die-hards are in the streets to pump up war fever, but the turnouts have been skimpy."

"Anything else?"

"Not for the moment, but we will be attending—in our own spy-like way—an emergency cabinet meeting early this afternoon. News at eleven."

"Thanks. Stay safe."

"Roger, that, Madam Vice-President."

The meeting of the UK cabinet that afternoon was stormy, to be euphemistic.

CHAPTER NINE

The roar of a large mature male lion on the African plains can be heard for five miles in the quiet of night. Shortly after he makes his deep-throated vocalization, lesser lions—male and female—respond from near and far. The sounds are enough to chill one's marrow. There was an indecipherable roar from inside the British Cabinet Room at 10 Downing that morning. Had anyone put his or her ear to the door, no separate or understandable words would be comprehended. But the mood and tenor of the shouting coming from inside the room would be unmistakable—fury and fight.

Inside the cabinet room, Lord Blancomb maintained his usual facial expression—that of a dead fish—with utmost effort and restraint. The PM was ranting and rambling, mostly incoherent. A majority of the other cabinet members interrupted as rudely and as often as they could to get their say said. Wood-Jackson would have none of it. His word was all that mattered, and he had no truck of fools. He won the place to convey his ideas by sheer dint of his profane vocabulary, his louder lion's roar, and his threatening gestures and tone.

Finally, a modicum of quiet and decorum settled over the room. PM Wood-Jackson cleared his voice, which was growing hoarse and looked with disdain around the room. Lord Blancomb tapped the button on his iPhone off mute and on record.

"You blatherin' east side idiots, none of you knows a whit about what is going on here and what has taken place. Shut yer gobs, and I'll tell you. You have fallen for an old American trick—leak to the press and let them convey the dictator's intended message.

"This is what is true: some American survivalists from the alt-left set off a few small bombs in the Naval Shipyard near DC yesterday. It caused a general panic like the Cousins are used to doing, and it got out to the whole world that someone—no evidence for who exactly—committed a huge massacre. It does not fit the dictator's message that it was those screw-balls on their pitiable left making another of their protests. Again, it was mostly African doers and white agitators using an old Jew plan. But, Weak Willets needed a better scapegoat; and, once again, he selected the United Kingdom, and blamed our military. Frankly, it would be a pretty poor lot of a military to have pulled off such a cock-up. Blimey, we could not have committed such a mess if we had set out to turn the mucking affair all to pot. What a bloody bunch of buggers those lefties were—couldn't tie their own shoes without government help."

"All they had to do is walk around quietly, plant three or four bombs, wire them up to a couple of cell phones, walk away and push a button, and Bob's yer uncle! They gave Weird Willets and Sad Sybil a perfect opportunity to switch the blame to us—after all *Pax Britannica* has done for those ungrateful blighters. Tomorrow we'll have a butcher's hook at the evidence.

"They have half their puny navy on the way to attack London. Let 'em come. They'll get what the Spanish got for their attempts with the Armada! Dismissed."

He raised both arms over his head, fists clenched— his signature campaign posture. The cabinet members applauded; some of them were near hysterical fervor; some were polite; and a few—like Lord Blancomb—were disgusted and distressed and kept their hands politely in their laps. No one, however, had the courage to offer a contrarian view or to bollock the raving maniac; and all of them fell into a line and walked out single file from the cabinet room like a flock of mindless lemmings.

PM Wood-Jackson's press secretary informed the nation that the PM was holding a war council in air force headquarters in High Wycombe and would be out of pocket for a week. In fact, the PM, foreign minister, deputy foreign minister, Lord Blancomb, the new First Lord of the Admiralty, and Her Britannic Majesty's Ambassador to the Russian Federation were ensconced in the Palace of Facets of the Kremlin having a serious conversation with Yankil Fedeorevich Naviensky, President of the Russian Federation.

Also present from the Russian side was Chief of the General Staff of the Russian Armed Forces, David Nikoliavich Porchenko, Pietro Maximovich Malenkov, the leader of the worldwide known *russkaya mafiya—Vorovskoy Mir* [Criminal/Thieves World]. *the* Vor (Thief), Papa, or *Avtoritet*, of the *Vory V Zakone* [Thieves by Law, the Authority which controls everything], and his sister and partner, Wanda Malenkov.

The British visitors had arrived in the Moscow International Airport in the middle of the night and were whisked off the large jet and onto a Kremlin a Mil Mi-8 helicopter. That conveyance avoided all contact with traffic and landed them in front of one of the out of the way Kremlin buildings. They gathered in a discrete office off the main throne room of the Palace of Facets located on Kremlin Cathedral Square. Security was discreet but very solid. Lord Blancomb had to turn his iPhone on and to place it in the box in the back of the room and hope for the best to get a recording.

President Naviensky made a quick formal round of introductions then said, "We meet here tonight at the request of our friend and brother in the struggle against the avaricious American hegemonists. It is his meeting; so, he shall state his interests and aims. Prime Minister Wood-Jackson:"

"We are having the same problems with America you are having; they want to run the entire world their way—the capitalist business way for their personal profit. They have been able to be the big bully since the Second World War. Look how it affects each of us. The UK cannot sail the high seas without those pirates boarding our ships for inspection or impounding them. Russia is under sanctions which hurt the economy because of your taking back the Crimea from those usurpers. General Porchenko, the mighty Russian military is stymied by the Americans who think they are the world's policemen. You can't finish the job you started in the Ukraine. And you, Pietro and Wanda; you can't travel anywhere freely without being subject to kidnapping by the American criminals.

"Enough!, I say, enough! It is high time we quietly joined together to interfere with the American colossus. I think we can sway Germany, maybe France, and easily get Italy, Spain, and Portugal, on board. You Russians should be able to 'incentivize' the former USSR satellites to be neutral at least. It's time to clip the wings of the American eagle!"

He recognized that he was starting to sound like a demagogue, like he did on purpose during his political campaigns. The voters liked it, but he realized that these great leaders were hard core realists and bombast was not the way to get them aboard.

"I'll stop while I'm ahead," he smiled, "I hope you realize that this is the time."

President Naviensky nodded to Vor Malenkov.

The Vor said, "My sister will explain our position."

Wanda Malenkov was a striking, statuesque tall blond with cold ice-blue eyes. You could say that she bore a significant resemblance to the American vice president, right down to the cold glance that could "thick men's blood with cold".

"We have anticipated this eventuality," she said, "it poses both problems and opportunities for the *Vorovskoy Mir*. The problems would come from a real war between the US and Russia that would eventually involve all our countries and organization. While there would be some human cost for the *Vorovskoy Mir*, the worst issues would be financial, coming from our loss of business revenue. Of course, if any of our people were arrested by the Americans, it would go hard for them and for our future. On the positive side, war is always a distraction, and always creates increased demands for our products and services. We will participate so long as the cost/benefit ratio is in our favor. Because the Americans will be heavily involved, there will be no question of betrayal on our part and switching sides."

She sat down.

President Naviensky next nodded to Chief of the General Staff of the Russian Armed Forces, David Nikoliavich Porchenko.

General Porchenko got right to the point, "We can protect our borders and can make life difficult for the Americans—give them a two front war if they are willing to go that far. The Russian Federation which my armed forces will benefit by gaining a free hand in the nuclear escalation, in being able to occupy the entirety of the

Ukraine, and the balance of military power will shift in our favor. The American presidency has weakened its military power by deserting Southeast Asia to the Chinese and has made enemies among all the European powers. We will once again have a strongman government for all the Russians without American interference."

"Thank you, David Nikoliavich. I concur with your salient observations. At the outset, we would only be willing to express our support for the UK's just cause. As the UK is able to attract allies and demonstrates its ability to succeed, we will take a more hands-on involvement, much like the French did in the case of the American-British War of the 18th century. On the negative side, we cannot afford all-out war with those American monsters; we have tested that possibility enough times to be sure of that. However, we can be part of the fleas that bite the dog—the fleas always win. Losing would wreck our economy and standing in the world for generations to come. We will not let ourselves get into that quagmire. On the positive side, there are tremendous possibilities. Remove American strength and reduce it to a 'once was' power, and a new world order will appear with the Russians being the alpha wolf. We will be at your side as soon as you make an internationally important statement, Mr. Prime Minister."

"I had hoped for more," responded PM Wood-Jackson; "but, I trust you, my friends, and I guarantee that the day you predict will come to pass."

He laughed, "But it remains to see which of us here is the alpha—the greatest among equals."

Lord Blancomb had to wait three days before he could get back to London and to dispatch the verbatim conversation back to Mac Young and Lincoln Howard. The coded and encrypted raw data was in Sybil Norcroft's and the president's hand the fourth day after the incredible meeting.

Prime Minister Wood-Jackson had another important meeting to attend before he returned to Number 10 Downing; so, he arranged for a second plane. Lord Blancomb decided to risk his career and possibly his life by having his trusted friend at MI-5 plant a voice activated listening bug into the PM's brief case. The well-known leader of the House of Lords was a sweaty mess as he waited for the PM's return or the nighttime knock on his home door.

The PM's meeting was held in Stockholm in a MI-6 safe house with no government members, even security present. Besides the PM, six men were present. Despite the near complete diversity among the men in the meeting, they all had one thing in common; they were once leaders of the Beelzebub the Magnificent's audacious plan to take over the world—which failed, but which left them extremely rich men with very highly placed contacts. They had a protective organization much like that of the Odessa which spirited important Nazis out of Europe at the end of World War II and found them fine and secure areas to semi-retire while they waited for the return of the much vaunted Fourth Reich. It would have been of supreme value to have had a "fly on the wall" in that meeting.

CHAPTER TEN

Prime Minister Wood-Jackson was never more at home, comfortable, and secure, than when he met his old cronies from his days at CATs Canterbury School for Boys and Eton. He did not have to play the buffoon or the great populist Pied Piper. He could slip into his natural Etonian accented speech and just talk. However–on this occasion–the talk was important. The five men with whom he was meeting were not only firm friends; but they had shared their good financial fortunes with Benjamin at several key points in his growing political career; and he owed them. It was reciprocal. Benjamin Wood-Jackson had literally saved their lives during the awful period of the Beelzebub the Magnificent witch hunt. He had given cover for the five meeting with him in Stockholm that morning and to five others with whom he would meet in the afternoon. One incautious word, and every one of them could end up in prison.

After a few mugs of rich dark brown Brawler Champion Ale, the milder [low alcohol, low hops] variety, to keep everyone cold sober, and a limit of ten old school stories, Benjamin clinked his fork on his mug.

"All right, you hottentots, listen up. I have become pretty busy if you haven't guessed, and I will have to leave in few minutes. Big things are brewing, and I want you to be part of them. I have a bit of a brouhaha going with the Cousins, and I am going to need some assistance. There's money in it for you; so, listen up. I need you and your contacts to get an effective rumor mill going all around the world that the American government is shaky and needs to invent a convenient little war to prop itself up. Its business economy is headed south. You are going to make those two statements self-fulfilling prophesies into reality. With my government's help, the stock markets on American products and services are going to make a stumble, in fact, several stumbles. Some phony incidences of US Navy acts of piracy need to get some traction in our friendly news outlets, suggesting that the US is so hard up for money that it is doing a little piracy on the side to sweeten its coffers. Invent some footage. Fake some big business failures."

"How long before you get to the part about what's in it for us?" one of the friends—a portly balding and red-faced Brit—asked.

"You will get a heads-up from my administration about impending news of business crashes, American ships sinking, and great new successes. You can work your stock wizardry to make money. But remember which hand feeds you; make sure that American businesses at least appear to be failing and that it is a growing trend—war jitters, that kind of thing. You are good at that sort of thing."

There followed a brief strategy meeting then a steak and kidney pie lunch. Benjamin Wood-Jackson was off to his next meetings: another high-level meeting with old Beelzebub cronies and a mid-level get-together with like-minded French, German, Italian, and Portuguese, co-conspirators.

Mac and Lincoln had managed to get day jobs at the Stockholm Brewery Pub downstairs from the meetings of the PM and his confidants, thanks to a heads-up from Lord Blancomb, their co-conspirator. They also managed to get good quality videos. All the intel they obtained was sent off to Sybil and the president before nightfall. Both the senior US officials assured the agents that letters of commendation were already in their CIA dossiers. That was not expected—just doing their jobs—but much appreciated. Good letters from the DCIA and the president were most helpful in climbing the ranks and better pay ladder.

President Willets looked thinner, sallower, and tireder when Vice-President Norcroft met with him after both had had a chance to digest the new intel. He was in the twenty-third month of his second term of office and looked as if he had aged a decade in the past two weeks.

"A little while ago, I would have thought that the worst thing I could learn was that there were still functioning Beelzebubers around the world. It's disconcerting. But, what we're seeing are plans for war—war against us by our most loyal ally, as I remember from grade school lessons," he said.

"And the news keeps getting worse. The Brits rammed our carrier, the *Langley*, with an old destroyer and sunk itself. Hardly even a dent in the Langley. But two of our destroyers were sunk by torpedoes from British subs," Sybil said.

"Sure the subs were British, Sybil?"

"All but certain. We hauled one destroyer off a sand bar and found a UK made fragment embedded in the hull. Serial numbers still clearly readable."

President Willets shook his head expressing his anger, sadness, and sense of futility.

"How is the blockade of London going? I've talked to the DOD, and they convey only good news; no ships escaping; no attacks on our carriers; and our planes are keeping theirs at bay, so far. What's your take over at the puzzle palace?"

"About the same. Seems that fear of a wipeout for them keeps the level-headed admirals and generals from unleashing World War III for the time being. Can't rely on good luck forever."

"What are you doing about this, Sybil?"

"Good that you ask. I do have a plan; but, Sir, I'm afraid it's above your paygrade."

She smiled.

"Meaning, it's better PR if I don't know, right?"

"You are such a smart president, Sir."

"Ummh hummh. Oh, I almost forgot. Bad news from my end. My cancer is not responding. I am coughing up blood almost all the time. My doctors won't let me go out in public...I hate to even say it, but they've given me no more than a month or six weeks to live. I will hang on for one more month before I let the twenty-second amendment be put into force. I won't be a nonfunctioning president like Woodrow Wilson for a day longer than I have to. But, Sybil, the terrible responsibility of this office is going to fall on you before you're ready unless we take time every day for me to give you all of the presidential secrets I am allowed to divulge before you are sworn in."

"Thanks, Mr. President. I know I should say some platitude like, 'there's always another treatment to try,' or just hang in there, everything will turn out fine. Doctors aren't always right,;' but you don't need a Pollyanna; and I respect you too much to act like one."

"Thank you for that. It's another reason I knew you had to be my veep. You have a friendly association with the truth, however unpleasant it is."

Sybil had her driver run her around DC for half an hour while she had a good cry in the back seat of the limo. When all of that was over, she ordered him to take her back to Langley. She did, indeed, have a plan. She was acting on a hunch and a presumption and knew that it could very well fail. However, the gathering storm on the high seas was stimulus enough to give almost any plan a try. The stakes could not be higher; it was not just a national emergency; it was a world emergency; and the world knew it. She called Landon Murphy, the DFBI.

"This is a secure line. Please give your personal Top-Secret ID code," the crisp voice of a strong woman's voice.

Sybil complied.

"Thank you, Madam Vice President. Director Murphy's voice will be the next on the line."

It was three minutes.

"Hi, Sybil, Landon here. What can I do for you?"

"Hi, Landon. I need your agents to do a favor for the president and me, and for the country, for that matter. You remember the Beelzebub matter, I'm sure."

"Of course."

"I need your agents to fly into Morgantown, West Virginia on the QT. Persuade the new CEO of

Morgantown Applied Linguistics and Media Development Center and three or four of his top scientists and program developers to come and meet me at my office in the Langley Building. I can't stress enough how secret this must be kept. Can I count on you?"

"Of course, you can. We have had a great and reciprocal relationship over the years, even bent a few rules together. Maybe this is one of those times, but I am aware of how serious everything you and I are working on now is. When do you need to see the visitors?"

"This afternoon."

"Well, then, we don't have any more time for idle chit-chat then, my friend. I'll get right on it."

"Thanks, Landon. And it is that important."

Lord Blancomb, First Lord of the Admiralty, met in secret with Air Chief Marshal Sir Percival Lindley-Jones, the CDS [Chief of the Defense Staff, professional head of the British Armed Forces], and Jacob Broz, senior advisor to the prime minister. The meeting was called by the PM to receive an up-to-date summary of the current defense situation and to convey the plans of the prime minister. It was understandably a very sober and all-business meeting.

The First Lord carried his handy iPhone ready for recording in an inner zippered pocket of his £7,000 custom tailored black Brioni windowpane wool-silk suit. His white shirt was stiffly starched, and his patterned red silk power tie was made by his tailors in Hong Kong. His handmade breathable black shoes were created for him by his cobbler on Saville Row. The three men sat facing each other over a small round hardwood table in the secure room of the royal air command at High Wycombe Air Base.

Sir Percival gave the situation report in terse military terms:

"Gentlemen, as of this morning, all is quiet. Tense, but quiet. Not a single shot has been fired. Zero casualties, even by accident. Washington will not speak to us. I have had a back-channel conversation with Admiral Fitzpatrick who commands the two US carrier groups mounting the blockade. It is my understanding that the Cousins do not want to shoot anything, but they cannot let the incidents in Norfolk, Virginia and in the open sea go by without some sort of serious reprimand—that was Fitzpatrick's choice of words. They have no plans of leaving."

"And what did you have to say to the nice admiral, perchance, Air Marshall?" Broz demanded; his tone barely civil.

"Fitzpatrick—who, incidentally, is an old friend of mine—asked in all earnestness, and I quote, 'What on earth possessed the British armed forces to obey such orders?'. His next question was, 'What do you plan next?' I did not have an answer for either of those questions."

"Sounds defeatist to me, and I shall so inform the PM as soon as this meeting is over. I am sure he will expect your resignation today. The situation is simple in one regard: you are either loyal to the PM, or you are not, whatever your opinion of lawful orders may or may not be. I will tell PM Wood-Jackson that you are not loyal, Sir."

Chief Air Marshall Lindley-Jones was dismissed that afternoon and placed under house arrest, but it took a full seventy-two hours to secure a new Chief of Defense. No UK General, Admiral, or Air Marshall, could be found to accept the position under the present circumstances; so, army Major General Archie Blamel was appointed as acting chief of defense by the PM. Wood-Jackson liked to have as many of his officers be "acting"; so, the officer reported only to the PM and could be hired or fired on Wood-Jackson's whim, leaving the rest of the government out of the loop.

A full verbatim account of the meeting was in the new acting DCIA, Martin Obershauer's, Sybil's, and President Willet's, hands before smoking lamp out time at the Pentagon, in the White House, and the Langley building.

The United States Navy carrier groups remained on high alert—DEFCON 2—in the English Channel and facing London from the Thames. No aircraft from either nation broke the implied interdiction in the skies, lest a white-hot conflict erupt due to some overzealous airman accidentally shooting off a round. Not so much as a fishing trawler or a pleasure yacht moved in the occupied waters. British naval ships were ordered to make to the nearest port. In all of history, there has never been such an uneasy quiet.

At the same time, an earnest meeting was taking place in the residence office of the vice president—Number One Observatory Circle, in the grounds of the United States Naval Observatory—to evade even the hint of suspicion that a game was afoot by having recognizable people file into the Langley CIA building under tight security guard. That was at the suggestion of the president. Sybil changed the locale plans accordingly. Only five people were in attendance in what would have appeared to be informal, had it not been for the very tight security—comparable to what would have been employed had the meeting been in the Oval Office. President Willets; his Chief of Staff, Gen. Omar Zabriski; Vice-President Sybil Norcroft; acting DCIA, Martin Obershauer; FBI Director Landon Murphy; George Q. Knight, CEO of Morgantown Applied Linguistics and Media Development Center, and his Chief of Operations, Kendall Ryan, were the attendees.

CHAPTER ELEVEN

M etropolitan Morgantown, West Virginia is a quiet family sort of place with a population of about 140,000 in a beautiful setting of trees and rivers. The people are friendly, industrious; and the city is welcoming to businesses. Among the most successful of those businesses is the Morgantown Applied Linguistics and Media Development Center. The center survived a scandal during the era of the manhunt for the self-dubbed Beelzebub the Magnificent. Back on its feet and concentrating on its legal business of applied linguistics, business had never been better. Consultations were sought from all parts of the commercial, educational, and governmental world.

The meeting taking place in the residence office of the vice president—Number One Observatory Circle, in the grounds of the United States Naval Observatory could be the nexus for a world altering historical change. The CEO and COO of the center would prove to be the most important figures in the making of history. Nevertheless, none of the august primaries in that meeting would ever be known for their role until the thirty-year statute of limitations for public revelation of classified information had elapsed, and then only if someone had some reason to ask, which was unlikely. Furthermore, most of the principles in the meeting would be dead before its secrets were revealed.

Vice-president Norcroft chaired the meeting and explained the problem facing the group of seven and ultimately the entire civilized world.

She was brief and to the point: "We must find a way to remove Benjamin Wood-Jackson from his place and influence as prime minister of the UK. He is creating a war to satisfy his own peculiar populist ambitions and cannot be allowed to persist in pursuing the danger he poses. I have an idea. It is not quite a moral concept, but it is by far the lesser of evils if it can be made to work. George Q. Knight, CEO of Morgantown Applied Linguistics and Media Development Center, and his Chief of Operations, Kendall Ryan, and I have discussed the basic concept of the plan. Their company can accomplish the technical elements, they assure me; then the rest of us—especially us spooks—will have the responsibility of executing the plan. Before any of the plan is divulged, everyone here will be required to sign the Official Secrets Act document with all its privileges and penalties—the latter being very severe. Not one scintilla of what is said or done today can ever be revealed to the public under penalty of treason."

Mr. Knight took the majority of the morning to explain the technical aspects of the project, a compendium of information that fascinated, excited, dismayed, and frightened, the rest of the people in the meeting. By noon, the rough outline of one of the most audacious secret actions ever proposed to a government were in place.

Prime Minister Wood-Jackson summoned the American admiral in command of the two carrier groups laying siege to a meeting at 10 Downing Street under a flag of truce.

Admiral Deacon Fitzpatrick scribbled a terse reply on the letter from Wood-Jackson, "No."

That reply from a mere American admiral was as confusing to the PM as WWII American Gen. McAuliffe's reply to the German general demanding surrender because the Germans had a commanding position, number of combatants, and firepower, over the American forces defending Bastogne. The reply from Brig. Gen. Anthony C. McAuliffe–both spoken and written was–"Nuts." The Germans spoke English, but the one-word reply was meaningless and confusing enough to become famous.

The British PM was livid, almost at a loss for words; but his fury enlivened him to a truly epic rendition of cursing in British English, American English, and German. He threw in a few Russian expletives for good measure. He was so enraged that he had to take to his bed for the next two hours. No one–but no one–had ever treated the arrogant prime minister that way. He vowed that a British attack would set to right the calculated insult.

Late in the afternoon, Wood-Jackson ordered an attack on the two carrier squadrons as soon as preparations could be finalized.

Lord Blancomb sat in his London office and debated what to do with the information he had received that the prime minister was, in effect, about to declare war—at least a de facto declaration—against the most powerful military in the world. He knew this would likely mean the end of the long and proud history of England. He struggled with the decision about informing his CIA contacts about that information and thereby making himself an even more committed traitor to the English government as it was presently constituted. He stepped into the secure room behind his office and typed in a message to the US agents. The message requested a meeting in one of the three usual clandestine meeting sites, this time on the benches in front of St Anne's Limehouse, the second highest clock tower in London.

Mac Young sauntered by first and reclined on the grass behind Blancomb's bench. Lincoln Howard paused by the bench to ask the time. He was carrying that morning's London Times. Mac moved closer to the bench and began to do a series of stretches and light calisthenics, obviously in preparation for a run.

Lord Blancomb bent over to tie his shoes and said in a quiet voice, "The attractive blond has decided in favor of attendance to the party tomorrow. She will be wearing her best opera gown."

He stood up, walked over to see the sign on the church's front doors, then walked slowly away without looking back.

As soon as he was out of sight, Mac and Lincoln hailed a black cab and rushed back to the safe house to send their message.

> To: DCIA, POTUS, VPOTUS, CJCS
>
> From: Agent 62-AZ7622B and Agent 70-AZ86KB
>
> Status: "Top Secret/SCI" level–access to specific sensitive compartmentalized information included below. Coded, eyes only, DCIA, POTUS, CJCS
>
> Best asset informs that No. 1 UK plans launch of full attack on US assets in the region next day. No public announcement as of this report.

POTUS was too ill to attend the strategy meeting in the situation room that evening; so, Sybil conducted the crucial meeting. The attendees included the same seven people who had met earlier in the day at the Naval Observatory plus the full JCOS and their deputies, the majority and minority leaders of the senate and the house and their deputies, the speaker of the house, the directors of all seventeen intelligence services and their deputies.

Sybil brought the assembled officials up to date on the status of the British v. American standoff.

"It would appear that the Brits intend something dramatic or even to launch an actual war sometime tomorrow, according to our sources in England. We have two carrier groups standing at DEFCON 2. Before I tell you more, I would like to hear from each of you. There are a lot of us here; so, limit your responses to a brief decision or suggestion of something new. However–before we begin–each person here must sign the National Secrets Act document agreeing to keep everything that is said or done today as a state secret, at least until the thirty-year statute of limitations expires. By then, most of us will be dead. Remember, that by signing you agree to abide by all requirements and that you understand that divulging information constitutes treason. You do not have to sign; but, if you don't, you must exit the room under guard and remain at house arrest without being able to have visitors or to communicate outside your home until the emergency is over."

Everyone signed; some more enthusiastically than others.

"Thank you," Sybil said. "We have worked through the day to bring a government plan to readiness. While we have gotten most of the work done due to the great work by our friends here, the CEO and COO of Morgantown Applied Linguistics and Media Development Center, and our own DARPA experts. What we are about to show you constitutes our main weapon for the early portion of the conflict. If the techs will lower the lights and turn on the iPad production, please."

The room grew dark.

It was late evening when the meeting adjourned. The vote was unanimous to choose Sybil's plan, even fraught with hazard as it was. She rushed to the White House residence to answer the president's request.

President Willets was lying on his back in his bed with foley catheter, IV lines, nasal O$_2$ cannulas, arterial line, and NG tube in place. He was pale, clammy, and wan; but he was alert and glad to see his vice-president, confidant, and friend.

"Thanks for coming, Sybil," he rasped.

"Of course, Mr. President."

"We need to send out some orders. You'd better do it since I am so weak for the moment that I'm not sure my mind is clear enough. Nobody needs to know how sick I am. My doctors tell me that I will perk up in about a week. I think the 22nd amendment action can wait until then. So, here's what I think we should do tomorrow morning first thing. The first boat or plane that menaces us anyplace or for any reason gets shot down as an example. Make it obvious that we are using restraint. Have the DOD and military assets all send letters to their counterparts stating that we have exercised utmost patience, but we cannot and will not tolerate action against us. Let it be known that we went to DEFCON-5-6 at midnight (tonight)."

"Mr. President, you are very tired; and now is not the time to burden you with a lot of details, but I have put into action a last-ditch plan to bring us back from the brink by getting Wood-Jackson and his base to come back to their senses. I want to ask them to hold off for a week so that you can meet his majesty on a neutral ship in mid-ocean for a collegial talk. When he gets there and you and I can be alone or nearly so with him, I can spring my surprise on him. I am convinced it will break the stalemate and dissuade him from making a dangerous or truly lethal mistake. Okay?"

"I trust you. And God willin' and the creek don't rise, I will be able to deliver the message myself with you at my side."

He began to fade then; so, Sybil slipped out of his room. She had a very busy night ahead of her.

CHAPTER TWELVE

Vice-President Norcroft had the US officials essential for war and those essential for espionage gather in the situation room. It was 0310. By O500, war plans were finalized—as a contingency should Sybil's plan fail. The president, veep, and new DCIA, were to be helicoptered to the deck of the British aircraft carrier, HMS *Queen Elizabeth*. It was one of two aircraft carriers of the United Kingdom's Royal Navy. She was commissioned on 7 December 7, 2017. She was surrounded by separate flotillas of US and British naval vessels and overflown by squadrons of fighter and bomber jets at close intervals. Since the battle of Midway, there had not been such an example of security at sea.

Prime Minister Wood-Jackson spoke to his senior naval staff in the commander's office in the Henry Leach Building and West Battery Building, HMS *Excellent*, Portsmouth, based at Whale Island, Portsmouth. It pleased him that he was safe for the moment in his own navy offices surrounded by the nation's best. It irked him no end that he had had to get permission from the besieging American Aircraft carriers because his launch could be the only ship given a pass in all of the waters near London and because he had to get permission from the arrogant wankers across the pond for the meeting that had been requested by Weird Willy Willets which was shortly to take place in the middle of the Pacific Ocean.

"I couldn't be happier if I was a puppy with two peckers," he said. "We have the yanks right where we want 'em. Think of the significance: they requested us to come to a meeting. They made sure that we were satisfied that the location was safe, secure, obscure, and to our liking—no negotiation even. I'd wager that none of you sea rats has ever even heard of the place: It's called Point Nemo after the submarine captain in one of our great English author Jules Verne's book, *Twenty Thousand Leagues Under the Sea*. The spot marks the center of an empty blue circle about the size of North America at GPS coordinates 48°52.6' south, 123°23.6' west. It lies 1,670 miles from three dots of land nobody ever heard of: Ducie Island on the north—an uninhabited atoll in the Pitcairn Islands; Motu Nui on the northeast—a tiny islet off Easter Island, which is off the coast of Chile—wherever that is—and a refrigerator sized dot called Maher Island to the south—off the Antarctic coast. Point Nemo is truly the most remote place on earth—more than 1,000 miles from civilization in all directions. If you want to find a place that is the 'middle-of-nowhere', Point Nemo is it.

"Anybody ever heard of it? Know anything about it?" he asked with a smug smile, knowing that his genius was about to be proved once again.

"Well, Sir, I know a bit about it," spoke up Lord Blancomb in his irritatingly calm and measured voice, "There is no human, and practically no biological life for a 1,000 miles in any direction—just open ocean. In fact, humans in space are far closer to the Point Nemo–which is known in the geographic and astronomy world–as the pole of inaccessibility. The astronauts aboard the International Space Station are around 258 miles from their home planet at any given time, closer than anyone on land. The word *"Nemo"* comes from the Latin for 'nobody.' That's altogether fitting," the First Sea Lord said, "since Point Nemo has never had a single visitor so far as anyone knows. The area is officially known to space agencies as the "South Pacific Ocean Uninhabited Area".

"Anyone else want to electrify us with his brilliance?" Wood-Jackson snarled out a challenge.

Admiral Mortimer Q. Nelson—sick of the antics of the self-proclaimed genius and well-known narcissist—spoke out anyway, "There's a bit more worth knowing. Sir. First of all, with Point Nemo at its center, the surrounding area of open Pacific Ocean is more than eight million six hundred fifty thousand square miles in size. You will be going to a compass point–not a speck of land–located in the South Pacific Gyre. That is a swift ocean current which washes away almost all nutrients in the water making it one of the most lifeless places in the world. About the only thing present there is pollution by plastic. One thing we learned from the yanks is that the Russian, European, and Japanese, space agencies have used it as a dumping ground for decades, because it is the point on the planet with the fewest human inhabitants and the quietest shipping routes.

"Over a hundred decommissioned spacecraft occupy this "spacecraft cemetery", from satellites and cargo ships to the defunct space station Mir. What's more, because the region is so isolated from land masses, the wind does not carry enough organic matter to feed anything. With no material falling from above, called–marine snow–the seafloor is also lifeless. As the First Lord pointed out, the only thing there is plastic—most of which was dumped there by trash ships from Japan, England, and the United States, and from space debris from falling satellites intentionally directed to that remote area."

"Enough of that climate change fake-news clap-trap. We have serious things—real things—to discuss. Now that you *tossers* have ventilated, sod-off, stop *whinging*, and let the big boys get on with business," the PM said to cut off any more discussion of things he did not understand or did not want to learn.

"This is what is going to happen in that meeting. First of all, the minute the talks begin, I will take charge. Perchance, you will remember how well I do that. My genius against their puny plans. I look forward for this meeting in the middle of the ocean to be remembered as one of the great events of the new world I will head."

The two delegations arrived on the flight deck of the *HMS Queen Elizabeth* an hour apart. It had been long and tiring, especially for President Willets, who was just beginning to feel a little better. His illness was counterbalanced by the seasickness suffered by PM Wood-Jackson. Everyone quickly went to his or her wardrooms and had a refreshing power nap.

The meeting convened in the Admiral's conference room which looked very much like the quality Admiral Lord Nelson had aboard his flagship HMS Victory. Because First Lord Blancomb had made the invitations, and because it was a British ship of the line, Blancomb made the introductions. All of the military officers from both the British and the American sides were in dress uniforms and medals, and the civilians were all dressed like toffs, except for Prime Minister Benjamin Wood Jackson, who was dressed in jaunty regatta yachtsman's summer outfit—khaki short shorts, red tee shirt with *"Pax Britannia"* embroidered on the front and his own full color facial photograph imprinted on the back. He wore comfortable old blue deck shoes with no socks. His hair needed a trim and was wind tossed; so, he looked like he just woke up at best or like a scarecrow in a cornfield at worst.

From the sky, it was a beautiful scene—light blue sunlit sky, cornflower blue ocean, and gleaming white ship. The sea was almost as calm as a mirror. From within the conference, it was tense to the point of approaching grim.

Lord Blancomb said, "Welcome ladies and gentlemen. I will take a moment to have each person introduce himself or herself, and his or her official position."

There was a quick communication of names and titles. The only surprise was when the PM spoke, which seemed a harbinger of things to come.

His statement was, "Prime Minister of the United Kingdom and all its land and sea domains, and soon to be the president and commander-in-chief of all the English-speaking peoples. I will be the Prince Royal of the kingdom bearing the title "First Prince of the United Kingdom and Successor to the throne in a new dynasty to be known hereafter not as Windsor, but as Wood-Jackson."

He said it without altering his serious facial expression, even though it clashed with his scarecrow corn silk thatch.

Every other person gritted his or her teeth to avoid even the hint of a grin or a frown or wrinkled brow.

"Yes," said Lord Blancomb blandly. "By prearrangement, the British side will speak first with the esteemed prime minister as first speaker. Then, the American side will be presented, with the first speaker being President of the United States, Parker Conrad Willets. Mr. Prime Minister…"

Each speaker was allotted twenty minutes to make his or her case. Wood-Jackson rambled on about a completely one-sided victory celebration and set of new world order commands for fifty minutes. No one from either side attempted to interrupt, to correct falsehoods, or to comment on the extreme nature of his demands—as if he were Mehmet II dictating complete surrender demands on whoever remained of the old Eastern Roman Empire after the defeat of the Romans in what was left of Constantinople in 1453.

The demands included: military surrender and transfer of all military equipment and weaponry to British control; transfer of all officers and enlisted personnel to the British command on land, sea, and air; and transfer of all intelligence officers, files, documents, and equipment to MI-5—and all forthwith.

Several jaws dropped, but facial expressions quickly returned to their previous soda-cracker unemotional expressions, as if they all collectively knew something the prime minister and next world emperor did not know.

When—at long last—it became President Willets' turn to speak, he was interrupted at the get-go by Wood-Jackson, who said in a stentorian voice, "Okay, Weak Willy, let's hear your *tosser* version. Be quick about it so we can get on with the real business—the transfer of power."

When Willets paused to determine if the boor had finished his rant, Wood-Jackson took it as a sign of weakness and an invitation for further commentary: "Stunned ye, did aye? I don't doubt that you are gutted and have lost the plot. But we don't have all day. Speak your piece and be done wi' it!"

Finally, Wood-Jackson decided that he had made an indelible impression—which was true—and he stopped talking.

President Willets nodded to the PM, "Ladies and gentlemen," he said, "Would all of you please exit the room except the prime minister, the first lord, the vice-president and me. We will need only a few minutes to convey our message. We have a presentation to make for the benefit of our British friends."

CHAPTER THIRTEEN

Out of curiosity more than anything else, PM Wood-Jackson held his piece waiting to see what the weak US president had in mind—some last-minute fool's effort—he presumed. There were only four individuals remaining in the conference room, five if you included the projectionist who had slipped into the room without attracting attention to himself. Wood-Jackson did not have time for the little people, and he ignored the man as he always did. Instead, he admired the beauty of the day. Looking from the port holes he saw a cornflower sea under a clear azure sky. The ocean was dead calm; there was no portent of storm on the horizon; and Wood-Jackson chose to consider that a good omen. He ran his fingers through his unruly hair in a vain attempt to put it into place. It had become something of a habit for him to do so, and he disliked being subject to little nervous habits which plagued lesser men.

It irritated him that President Willets did not begin to speak. He was obviously waiting for the projectionist to get his work done. The man set up his equipment, plugged the several elements into wall sockets, set up a large viewing screen, and tested to see that the light hit the screen squarely.

The projectionist nodded to Vice-President Daniels—having been reminded that she preferred to use her husband's family name since assuming the office.

President Willets began to speak. Everyone had to pay close attention because his voice was muted and hoarse. He enunciated clearly and spoke slowly so that his every word and meaning would be comprehended.

"I will be brief. For the benefit of our esteemed Prime Minister Wood-Jackson, we have brought in some evidence in the form of digital videos."

Immediately the screen lit up with a series of short–but astonishing–videos in which British Prime Minister Benjamin Wood-Jackson was the lead actor. Each video was remarkable for how clearly Wood-Jackson was shown and heard.

The first showed him meeting with President Xi Yuen Lee, of the People's Republic of China listening to the PM telling him about the requirements for China to deal with the Russians and how pleased Beelzebub would be when they had completed their assignments.

The second revealed Wood-Jackson whispering to his chief aides about how to destroy an opposing candidate in the upcoming election, including the use of forceful intimidation.

The third showed the PM accepting a generous bribe from a Russian oligarch to swing a vote against censuring Russia.

The fourth revealed the PM involved in a love triangle with two well-known British gays.

The fifth was the best production. The PM was shown giving orders for attacks on American ships and receiving a hefty bribe from one of Great Britain's largest weapons manufacturers.

The projection stopped; and, for a moment, the room was silent.

Then, British Prime Minister Benjamin Wood-Jackson screamed—literally screamed—LIES! FAKES! FICTION! A DIRTY SMEAR!"

His face was purple with rage. His teeth chattered— the portent of those few videos was self-evident. He knew that if he could not discredit them, he was finished.

He looked President Willets and Vice-President Daniels directly in their eyes, "I will be able to have our good British experts find how and where this crap was fabricated. You will play the buffoon then, Wild Willie and your lapdog Sick Mind Sybil. You can't take me down that easy!"

Everyone else in the room waited until the tempest re-entered the teapot.

When all was once again quiet, Sybil spoke in her iciest quiet voice, "Ben, you are dead. All that is left is to lie down. But you need more proof to convince you. Please turn on the projector again. Run Video twenty-five."

She had captured the PM's attention. He could not imagine what more there could possibly be.

Video twenty-five had all the clarity, excellent sound, and vivid color, expected from a Hollywood sound stage. It was thirty-one minutes long.

Sybil enjoyed every minute of it, even though she had seen it dozens of times—the PM not so much.

The video opened with a group of portly pot-bellied men sitting in a sauna room with wisps of steam wafting around them. They were having a ribald conversation about their rich lore of sexual conquests. The men included six of the major figures in the Conservative Party, plus their hand selected prime minister. When it came his turn to talk, Ben Wood-Jackson first looked around furtively as if to detect any unauthorized listener. Then, he spoke in low conspiratorial tones and told of conquest after conquest of pre-pubertal girls. He explained in explicit detail the source of supply of those little girls—a special unit of the SVR RF [*Sluzhba vneshney razvedki Rossiyskoy Federatsii, IPA*] which was the successor of the PGU [First Chief Directorate] of the KGB. He became more enthusiastic and laughed out loud when he uttered the damning sentence:

"Talk about your win-win. This was my little payment for arranging for the Russians to have clearance to hit the Chinese sub. And there's plenty more where they came from. Anyone want in?"

Several of the very well-known political figures showed their enthusiasm for enjoying the treats. It had taken Sybil several viewings before she could see it without retching.

"OUTRAGEOUS FAKE!!!" Wood-Jackson shouted at the top of his lungs. FAKE NEWS! FAKE NEWS! FAKE NEWS!"

"Shut up, you creep," Sybil said quietly and venomously. "There's more. Save your protests until you see the rest. This is only a teaser. We have a total of one-hundred-twenty-one of these—all extremely entertaining. We have trailers for each. We have contacted the editors of every major newspaper and television outlet in the UK to arrange to show them during prime time over the next six weeks—seven days a week when the kiddies are in bed. Then, they will begin running the unedited complete videos all day every Wednesday for 121 weeks. Math is not my strong suit, but I do know it comes out to a lot of weeks. The new, noncorrupt, non-dictatorship, government has all the evidence from these videos. You may be surprised to know that they showed significant prosecutorial interest."

The "more" Sybil indicated included three addenda to the main video: First—a good quality motion picture of Vladimir Putin congratulating Wood-Jackson on his choice of "business partners"–referring to the Armenian Mafia–who he said worked so well to provide the "stock" for the thriving enterprise. Second—a conference room—the official conference room—filled with Conservative Party senior officials and seventeen senior military officers of the Royal Armed Forces. An overheated Benjamin Wood-Jackson—in a rambling rant screaming orders all around to attack specific military targets of the United States including bombing of Norfolk Naval Shipyard, and selected ships of the line. Third—a cabinet meeting wherein the prime minister outlined the overthrow of the Windsor monarchy in favor of a president-for-life government with all other departments being subordinate to the power of the executive. Wood-Jackson is identified by name as that president-for-life. Queen Elizabeth II was characterized as a wanker, a bleeding liberal, a frumpy fanny, a dodgy, freaky old broad, and a host of other vivid depictions not fit to print.

The Brits in the room paled and were aghast. Except for Benjamin Wood-Jackson—who had finally realized that the jig was up. He began to cry.

"So, what now?" he managed to croak out.

"A couple of choices," President Willets answered.

It was evident that even speaking was very tiring. He looked to Sybil for assistance.

She said, without mincing even syllables, "This is what you will do starting as soon as we walk back into the Admiral's wardroom. Here is a written statement you will read to the assemblage. You will read it verbatim and will swear that you were not coerced or threatened. Note that you are resigning your position as prime minister and as head of the Conservative Party due to family health problems. If you do as you are told, nothing you have seen or heard in this room needs to see the light of day—ever. You can go to your stateroom and have a good cry or whatever. From this moment on, you are under detention by the Royal Navy under the command of the First Sea Lord. You are on suicide watch.

"When we pass Apra Harbor and stop at Naval Base Guam, you will be transferred to a comfortable United States Air Force jet headed to Virginia, USA, where you will be given a very educational tour."

"You mean where I'll be tortured and murdered, with complicity by the Royal Navy; that's what you really mean."

"No, Sir. I mean exactly what I said. I suggest strongly that you do not verbalize until we reach Virginia. Then–under orders by the president–you and I and the First Sea Lord will take a short trip. After that, you will be delivered to your home where you will receive further instructions. My personal preference is that you be hanged, drawn, and quartered; but neither we nor the British do that anymore."

During the long flight from Guam to Norfolk Naval Air Station, Lord Brancomb had an opportunity to query Sybil about what had happened.

"My friend," she said, "what I am going to tell you will have to remain a state secret in perpetuity on both our parts. I am going to tell you because you and I are friends, and I trust you. Furthermore, I suspect that we will have a lot to do with one another."

She then told him of the plan she had hatched to bring down the wild "off the hizzle" kamikaze of Britain—her characterization. She explained the role of Morgantown Applied Linguistics and Media Development Center who manipulated the utterances, facial expressions, lip movements, and bodily mannerisms, of the characters shown in the videos. The videos would appear to be genuine to any expert except a very few applied linguists scattered around the world. She told Lord Brancomb how she and several other members of the Company were impressed enough by what they had learned in the Beelzebub case to engage the Morgantown firm in a secret project to be able to create almost any scenario they desired to produce. She was convinced that her work had convinced Wood-Jackson that further resistance would be futile—that she and President Willets had won, and he had lost. His protests would fall from his disgrace upon deaf ears of the furious citizens of the world.

Once–when she had taken a university political science class for a tour of the CIA building–Sybil was asked whether or not she always told the truth in her position as DCIA. Her reply had been at that time, "Of course not. It is my job to lie for my country."

She had cause to reflect on her recent actions as the puppeteer-in-chief in dealing with Prime Minister of the United Kingdom. She recognized that over her years of government service, she had developed a rather different moral compass. That was evident to her since the potential war with England, and her role in it, because she had no sense of guilt. In fact, she was looking forward to giving Benjamin Wood-Jackson a memorable tour.

She, Wood-Jackson—who was blindfolded before they landed in America–and Lord Brancomb, flew into Andrews Air Force Base and transferred to a small Lear jet for the flight to the Farm [CIA training center in Virginia]. No one saw any of them enter the first plane in Guam, the second in Washington DC, or their entrance into a supermax, ultra-secret federal prison hidden in a wild grove of trees.

"So, liar, this is where it happens. Do I get to say any last words, tell my boyfriend that I am going, or let my party know that I kept the faith to the end?"

"Save the theater for someone who cares," Sybil said rudely.

Once inside the tomb-like facility, a guard removed the black hood and then placed wrist, waist, and ankle shackles. Accompanied by six silent guards—all large and taciturn men and women—marched down to the lowest level, then along a dimly lit corridor. Only the featureless cells had lights, just sufficient for guards to maintain suicide watches on the lifers in the cells. They entered a narrow corridor behind the row of cells and looked through one-way mirrors at the occupant of cell number B-1X. The man was neatly shaved, and his hair short and neat following his bi-weekly haircut. He was instantly recognizable.

Former Vice-President Randall Broome-aka Beelzebub the Magnificent–sat on a straight-backed metal chair staring at the blank mirror. He wore a blaze orange paper jump suit with no belt, buttons, or strings, and paper shoes. His expression was as blank as a paper mâché mask and as devoid of color.

At a nod from Sybil, a disarticulated voice made Broome jump in surprise, "Standup."

He stood like a robot, turned slowly full circle, and sat down again.

"Show your tongue and teeth."

Broome complied robotically.

"Stand in front of the mirror face on, then left profile, then right profile."

Again, compliance was immediate.

Sybil nodded again, and the light dimmed significantly in the cell.

"Now, Ben, you have options. You can live out your life in an adjoining cell, or you can live in your mansion outside London with severe restrictions. It all depends on what you say and do starting today and for the rest of your life. Option one will result from any deviation from the silence rule demanded of you. Option two will result from you living out your life by being an actor in a play. Shakespeare said that 'All the world's a stage, and all the men and women merely players; they have their exits and their entrances.' You play the role of invalid and presumably disgraced demagogue carrying a secret of an evil life that no one else can know about. Your public life is over. Choose now."

"I presume I'll be watched constantly," Wood-Jackson said.

"You are a perspicacious sort of a fellow. Never forget the lessons of the last few days."

Benjamin Wood-Jackson was many things: He had a serious personality disorder—sociopathic, greedy, lacking in sympathy and empathy, narcissistic, and mean; but he was not stupid. He would remember the lessons and the teacher to his dying day.

Sybil, her husband, daughter Cerisse, her husband Drake, and their two toddlers, flew to a secret getaway place in the Uintah Mountains of Utah. For five days, they swam, sunbathed, overate, hiked, laughed, and frolicked, as if they were like other people.

That misperception quickly evaporated when two marine helicopters landed in the field in front of the rude log cabin where those regular folks lived.

Four large men in matching black suits, white shirts, black ties, and black shoes walked briskly up to Sybil. They had several characteristics that were same for all of them. They wore serious expressions, sunglasses, and had bulges beneath their left armpits under their suitcoats.

"Madam President, we come bearing bad news. President Willets died during the night of pneumonia. Pursuant to the Constitution, you are now the President of the United States. Please come with us in the first chopper, and your family in the other. We will keep you safe."

Sybil Norcroft Daniels was speechless, then humiliated, by being unable to staunch the flood of tears that flooded down her sunburned cheeks.

-THE END-